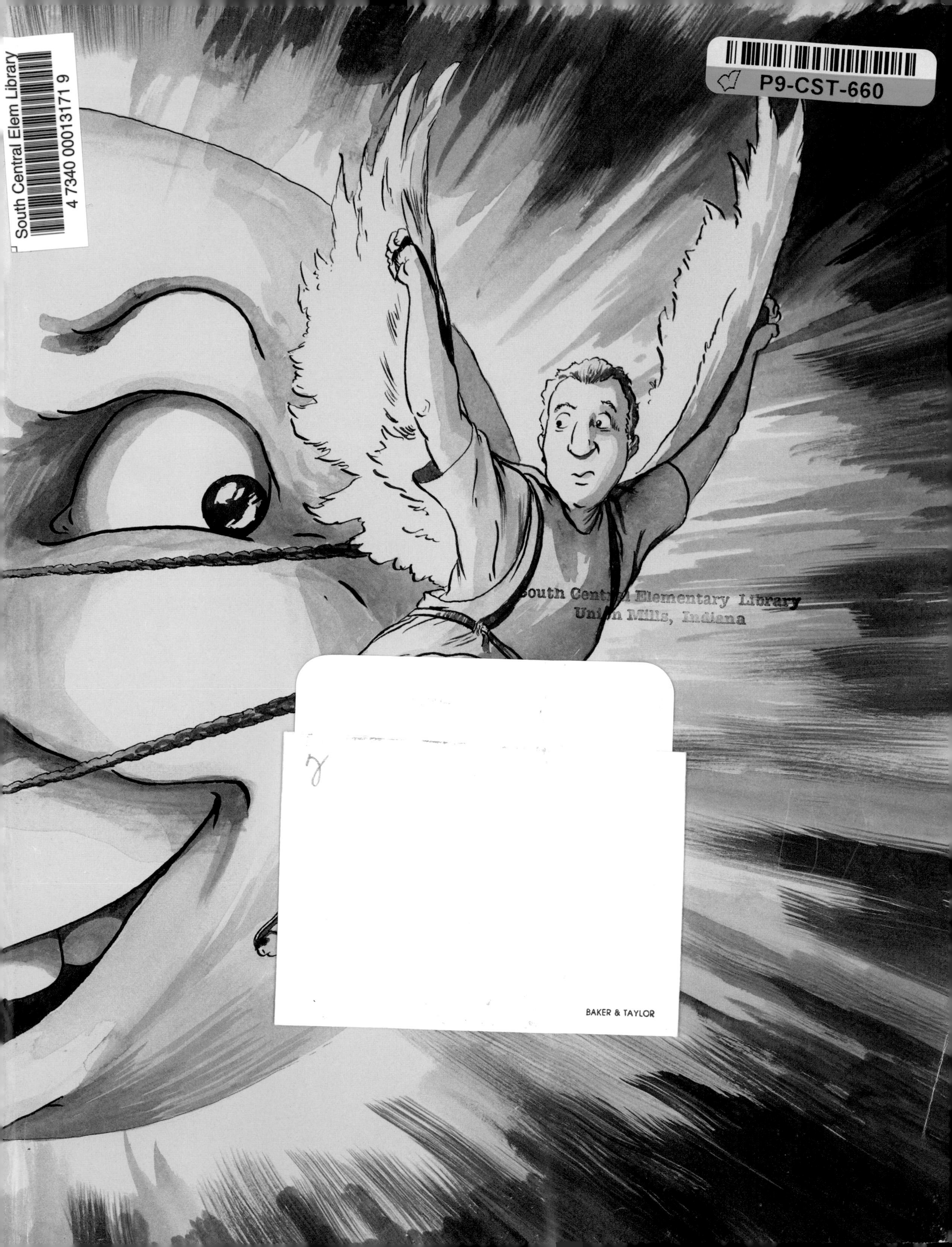

Fresh off their win over the Titans,
the Gods are riding high—
but those always-pesky Mortals think they just might be able
to bring them crashing to Earth.
It's gonna be a Grecian battleground,
a Mediterranean meltdown . . .
and you'll see it all here tonight on . . .

For Winsor McCay

First published in the United States of America in 2003 by
Walker Publishing Company, Inc.

Published simultaneously in Canada by Fitzhenry and Whiteside, Markham, Ontario L3R 4T8

For information about permission to reproduce selections from
this book, write to Permissions, Walker & Company,
435 Hudson Street, New York, New York 10014

Library of Congress Cataloging-in-Publication Data available upon request.
ISBN 0-8027-8844-0 (hardcover)
ISBN 0-8027-8845-9 (reinforced)

The artist used acrylic paints on 110-pound watercolor paper to create the illustrations for this book.

Book design by Sophie Ye Chin

Visit Walker & Company's Web site at www.walkerbooks.com

Printed in Hong Kong

2 4 6 8 10 9 7 5 3

Mount Olympus Basketball

KEVIN O'MALLEY

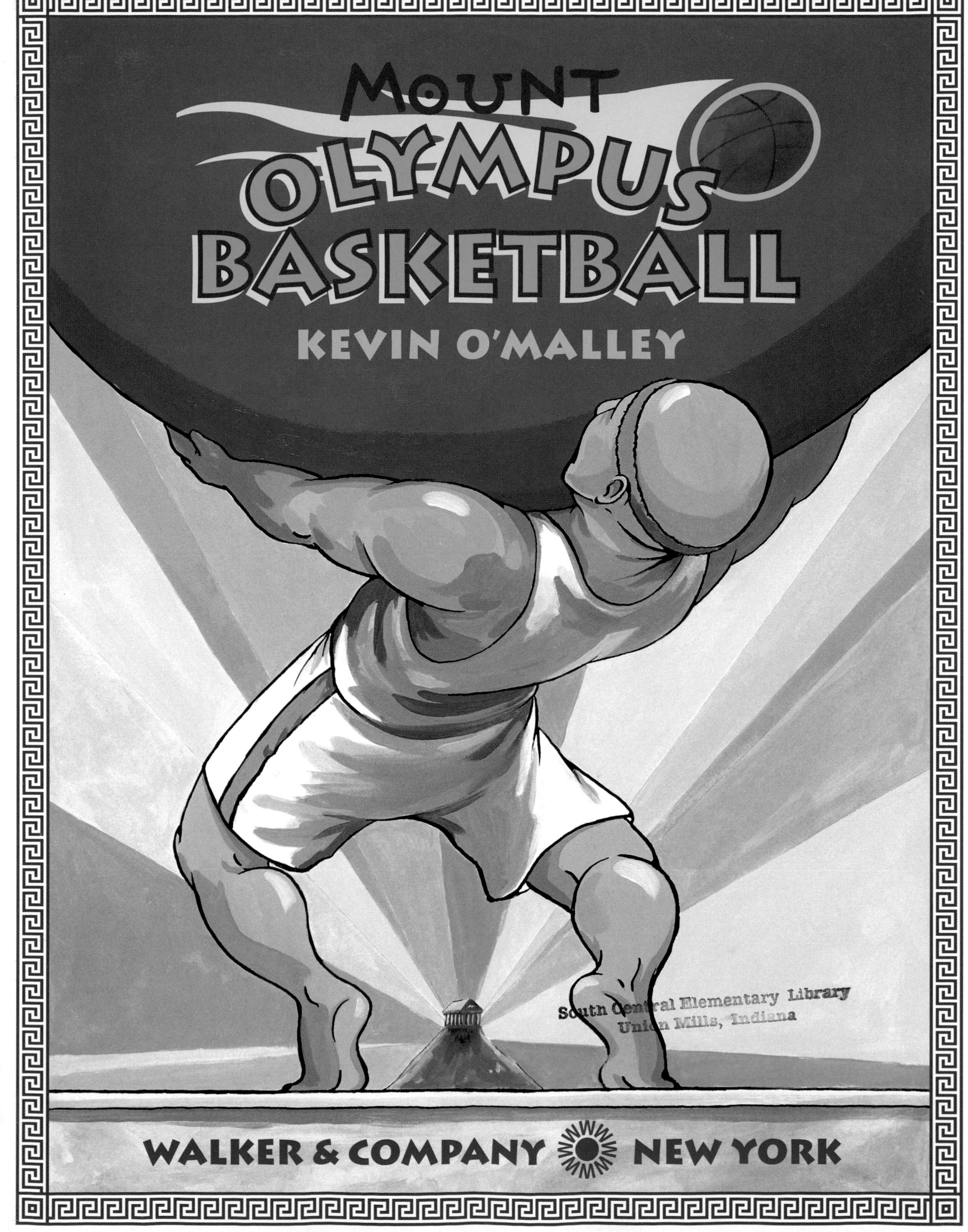

WALKER & COMPANY NEW YORK

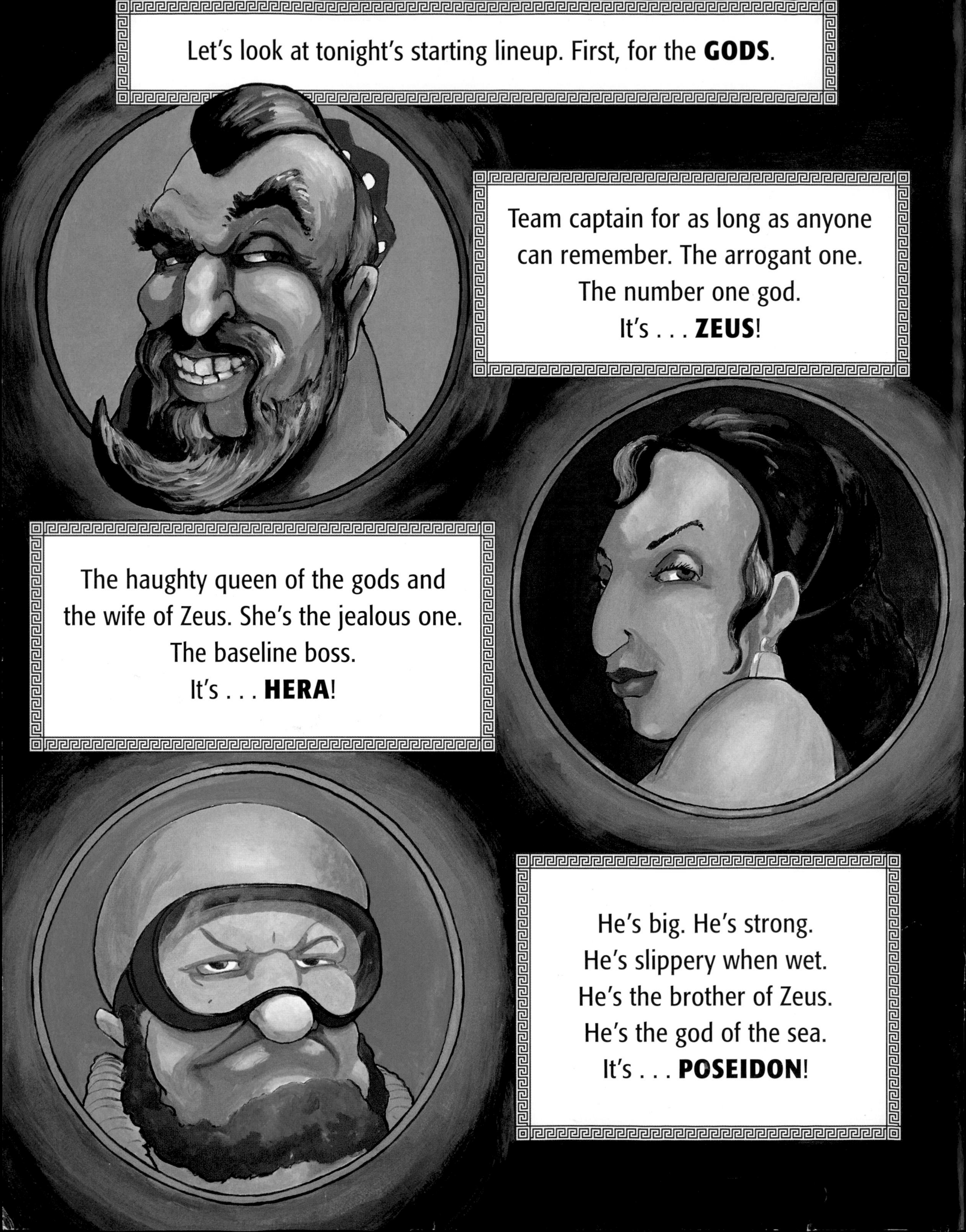
Let's look at tonight's starting lineup. First, for the **GODS**.
Team captain for as long as anyone can remember. The arrogant one. The number one god. It's . . . **ZEUS**!
The haughty queen of the gods and the wife of Zeus. She's the jealous one. The baseline boss. It's . . . **HERA**!
He's big. He's strong. He's slippery when wet. He's the brother of Zeus. He's the god of the sea. It's . . . **POSEIDON**!

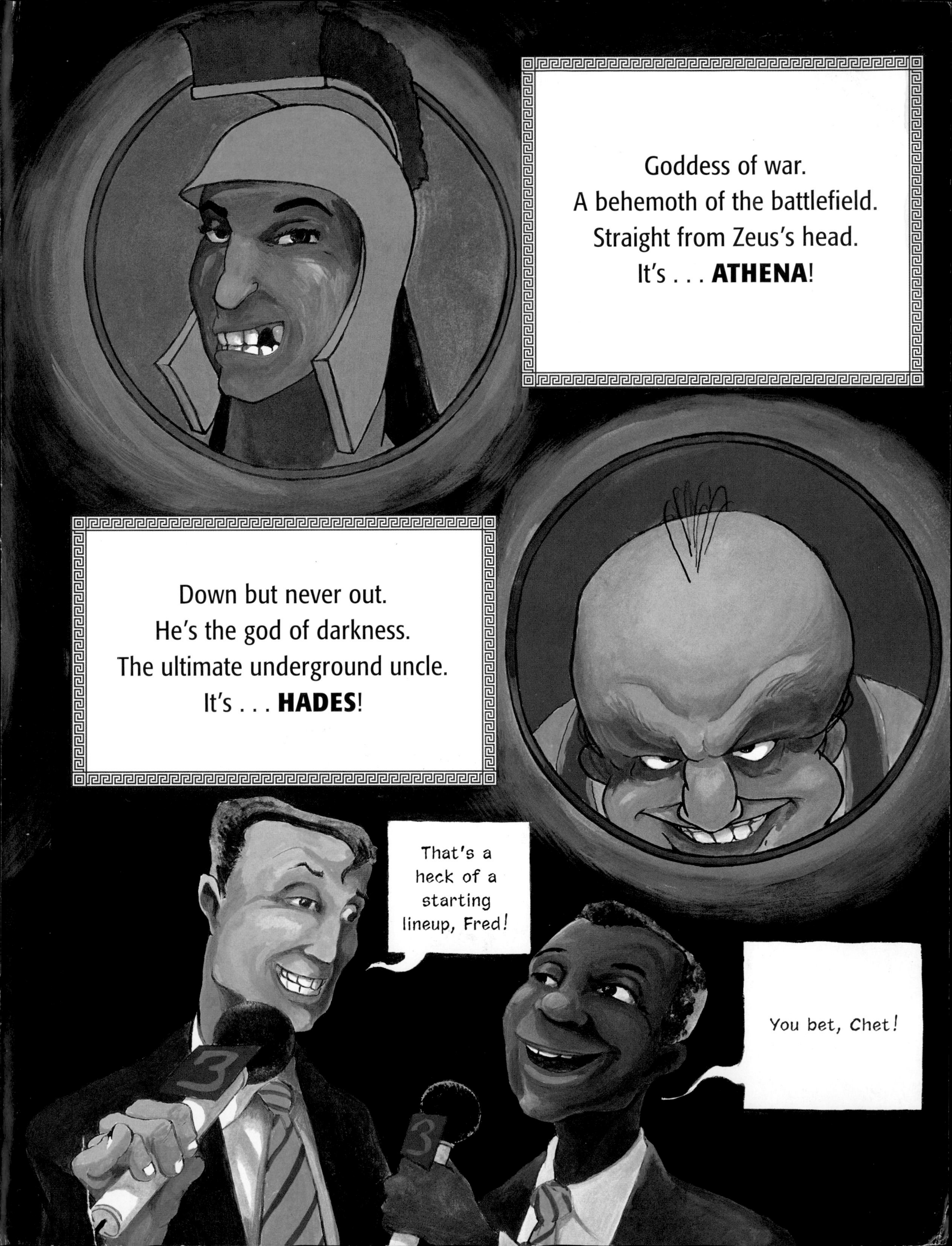
Goddess of war. A behemoth of the battlefield. Straight from Zeus's head. It's . . . **ATHENA**!
Down but never out. He's the god of darkness. The ultimate underground uncle. It's . . . **HADES**!
That's a heck of a starting lineup, Fred!
You bet, Chet!
3
3

On the other end of the court . . .
those crazy kids from planet Earth . . .
the mighty **MORTALS**!

Toiling tirelessly at
twelve tough tasks, he's the hero
and heart of humanity.
It's . . . **HERCULES**!

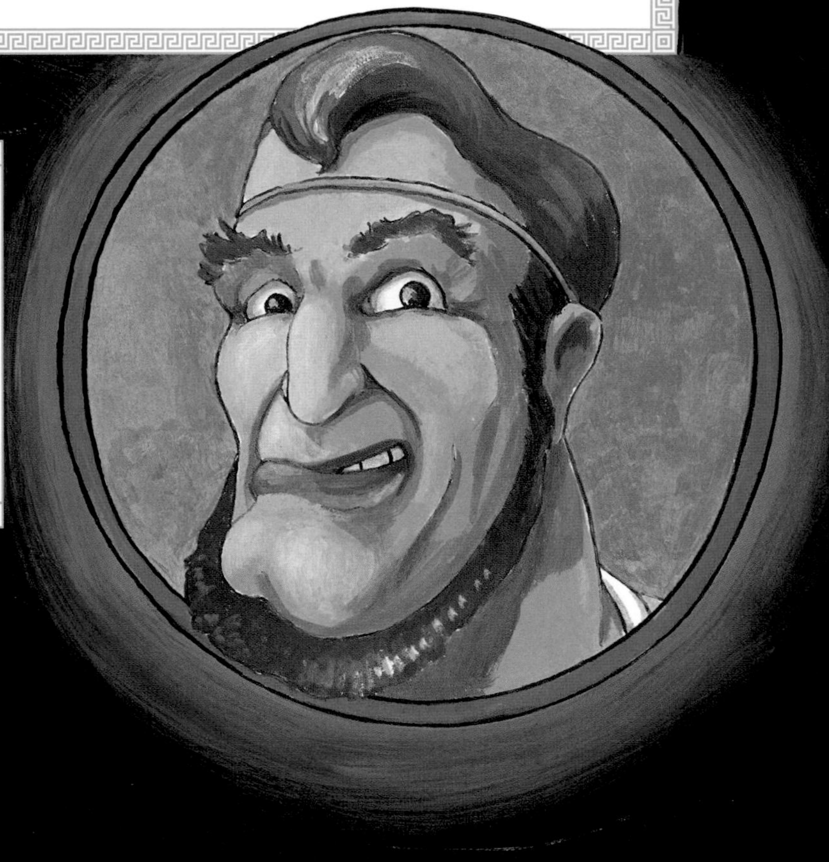

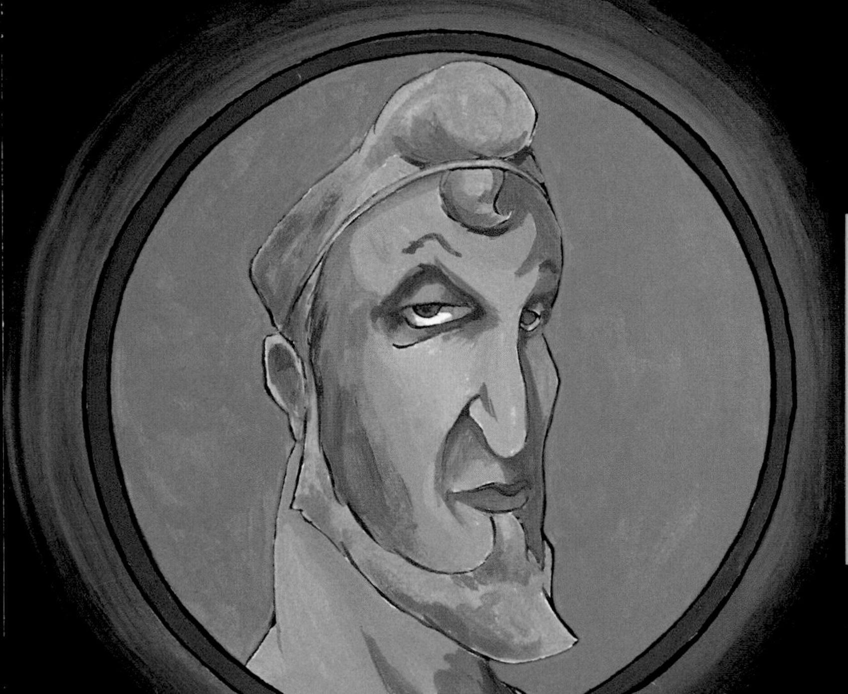

He's just back from surgery
on his heel
and begging for a fight.
It's . . . **ACHILLES**!

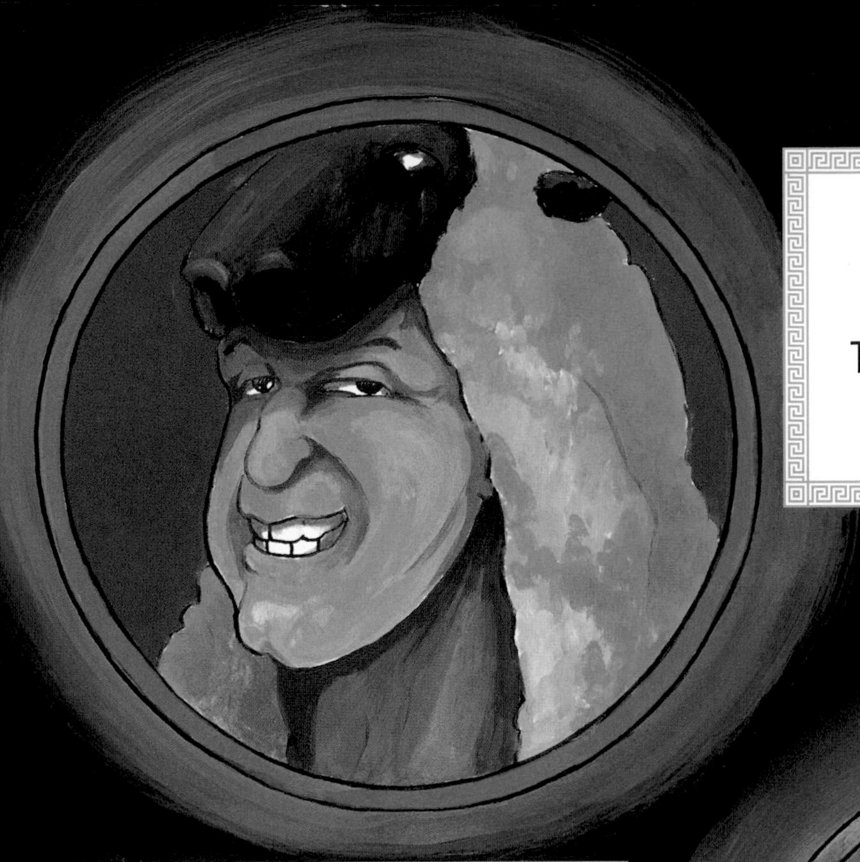

The golden boy.
The slayer of serpent-dragons.
The keeper of the Golden Fleece.
It's . . . **JASON**!

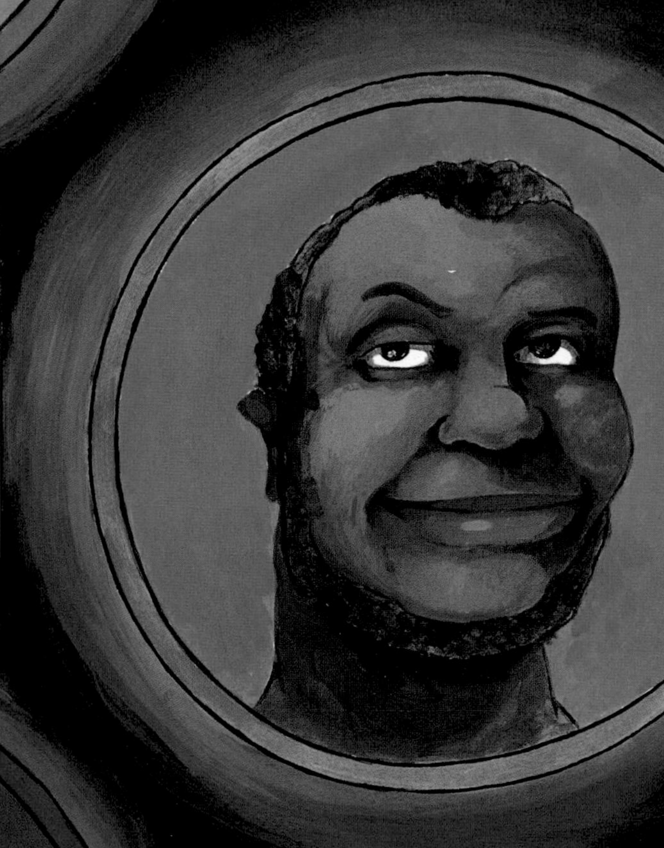

He's clever.
He's crafty.
He's just *AAAA-MAZING!*
It's . . . **THESEUS**!

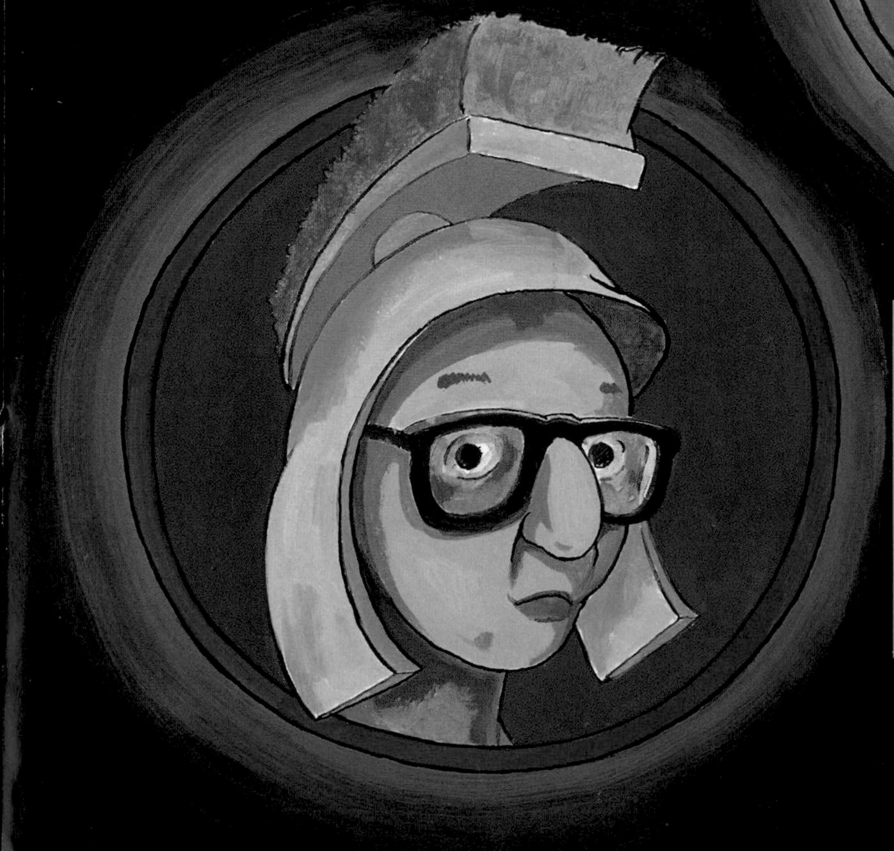

And last but not least,
the reluctant but heroic hero
in last week's Battle of Troy.
It's . . . **ODYSSEUS**!

Chet, look for Hercules to have a big game tonight.
He's looking stronger than ever.
And I talked to Jason. He's just back from overseas.
He said the Argonauts held up okay.
By the looks of them I'd have to agree.

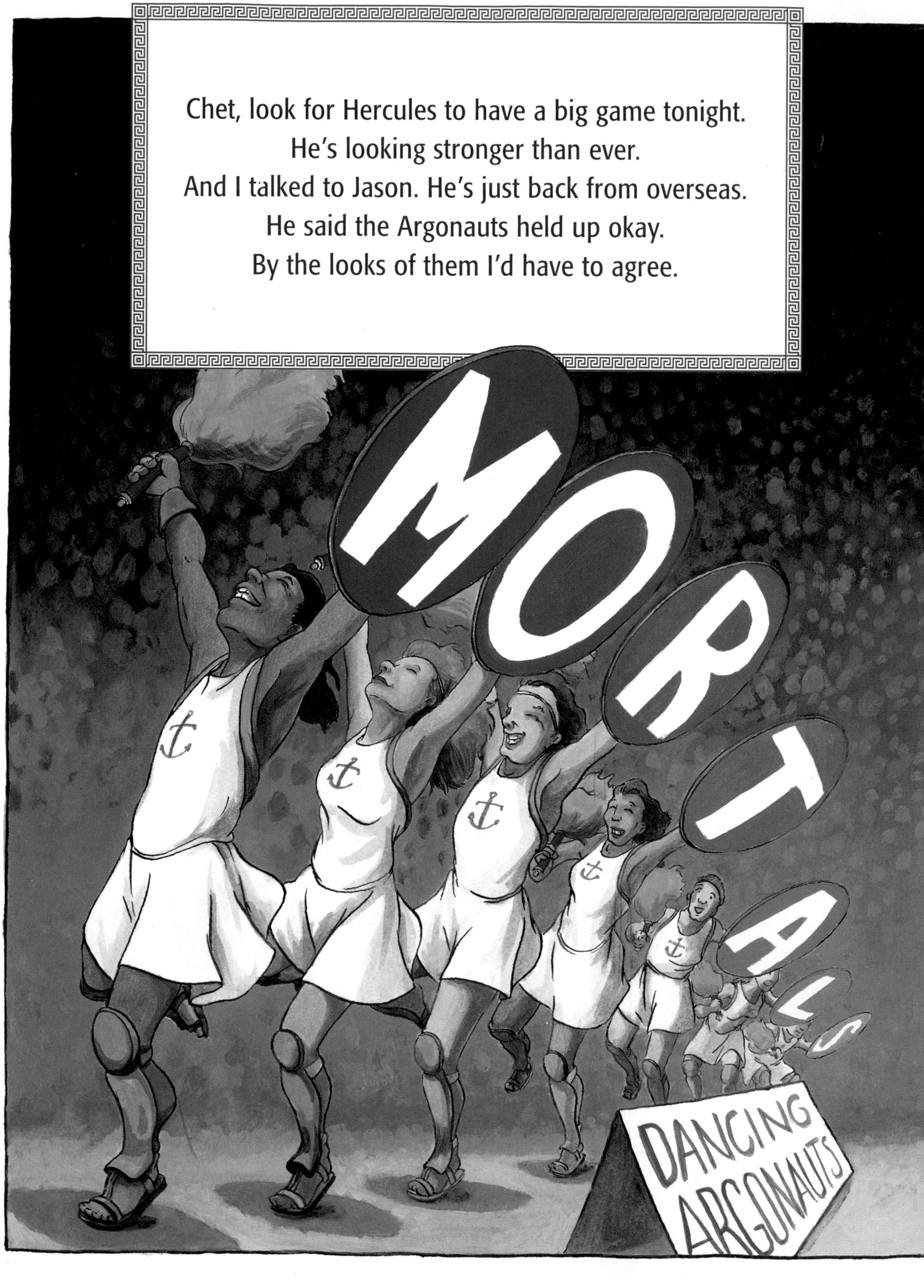
MORTALS
DANCING ARGONAUTS

Well, here's the tip-off.
And at the start of
tonight's game, as usual,
Zeus controls the ball.

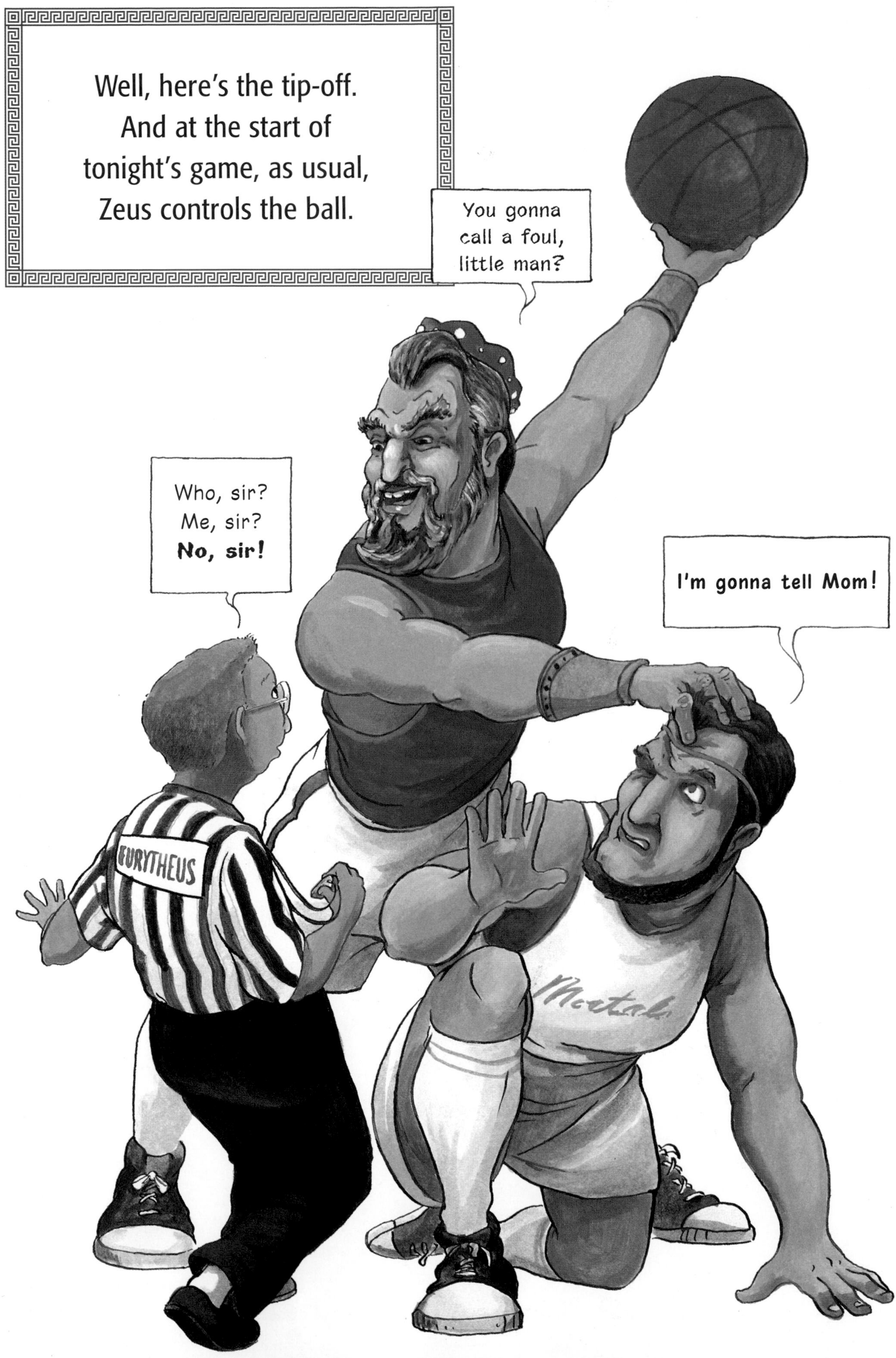
You gonna call a foul, little man?
Who, sir? Me, sir? **No, sir!**
I'm gonna tell Mom!
EURYTHEUS

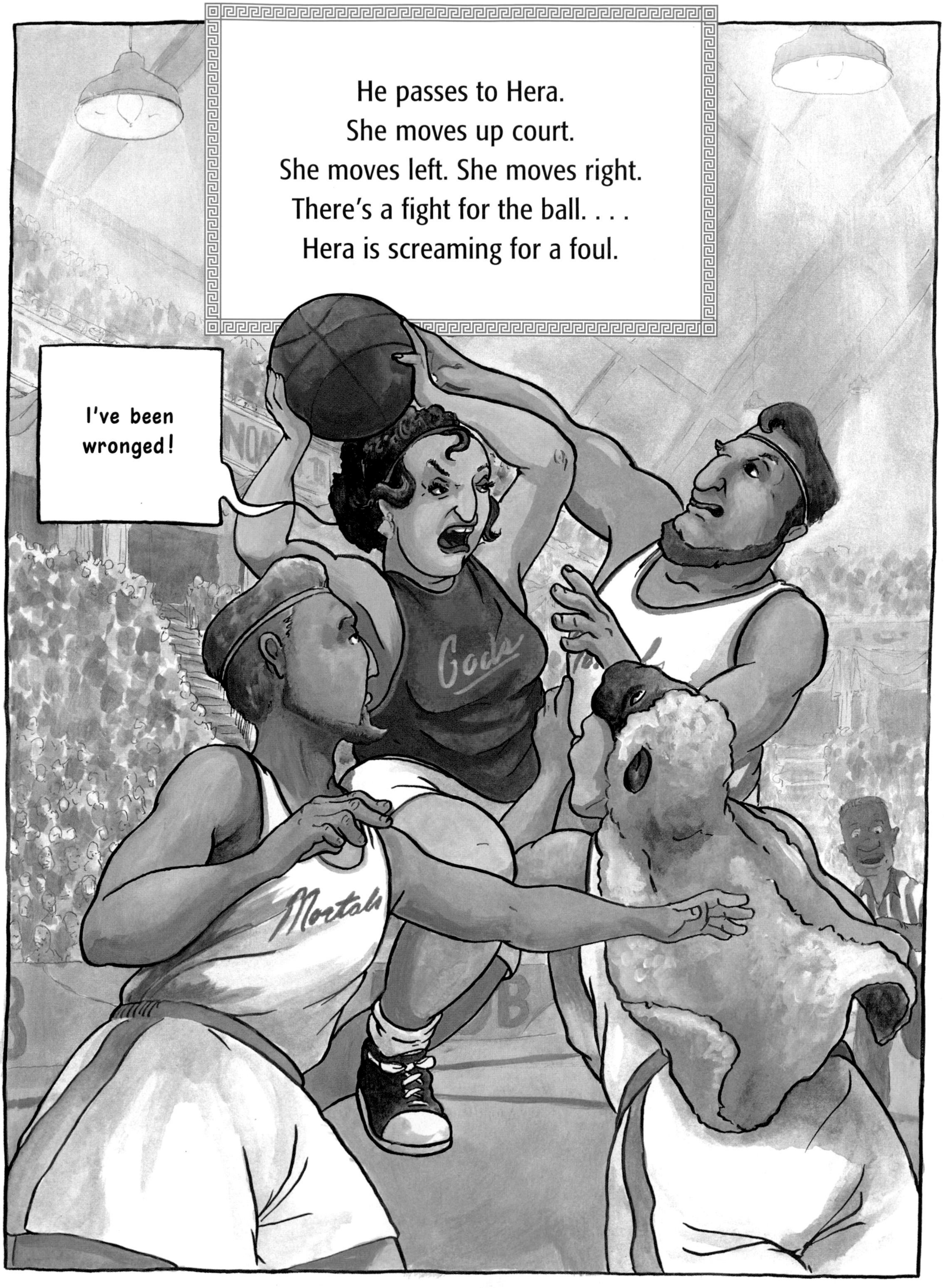
He passes to Hera.
She moves up court.
She moves left. She moves right.
There's a fight for the ball. . . .
Hera is screaming for a foul.
I've been wronged!
Gods
Mortals

When Hera is mad . . . look out!
The ref has awarded the Gods two points,
but it's too late.
Hera has turned him into a cow.

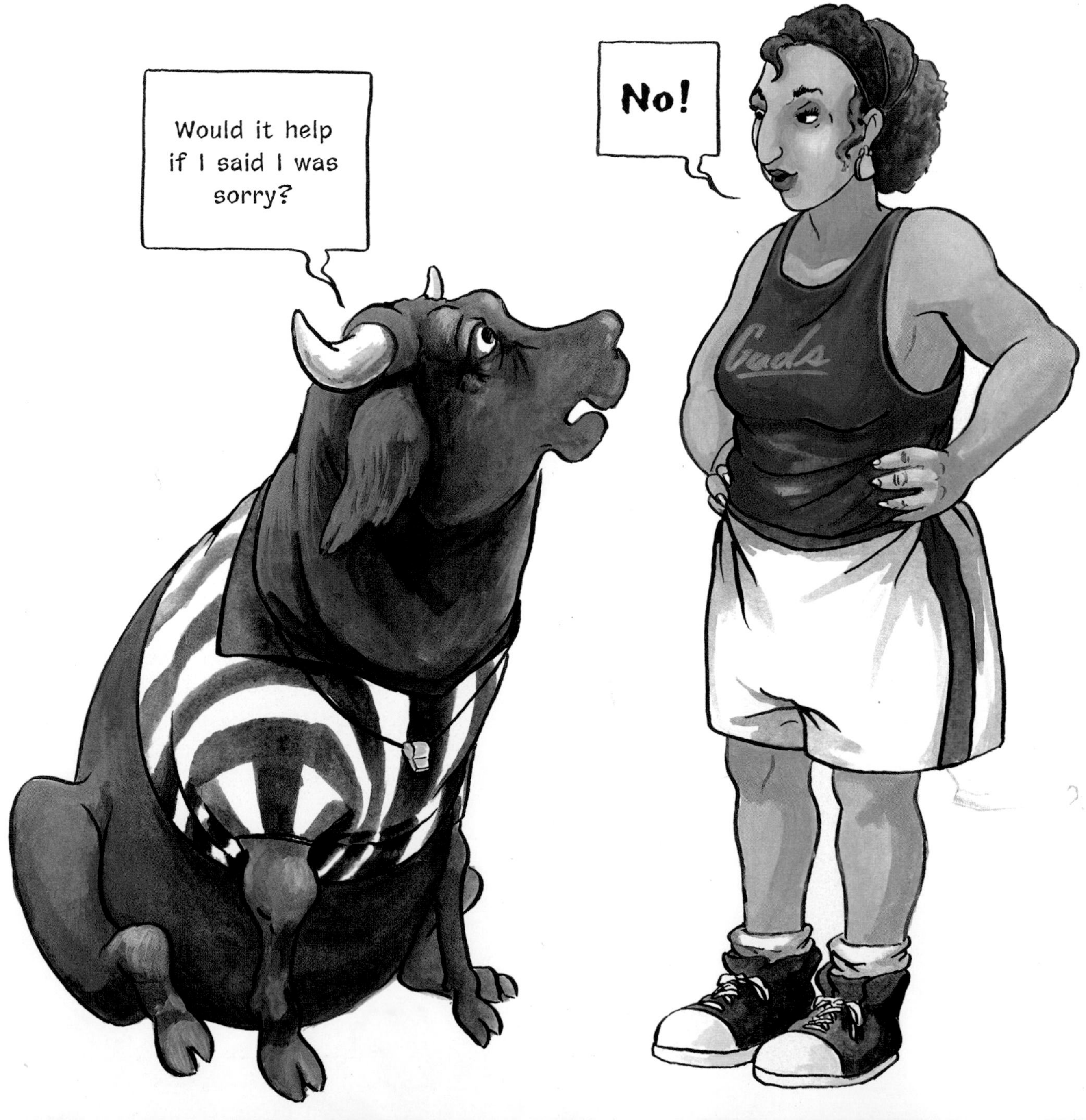
Would it help if I said I was sorry?
No!
Gods

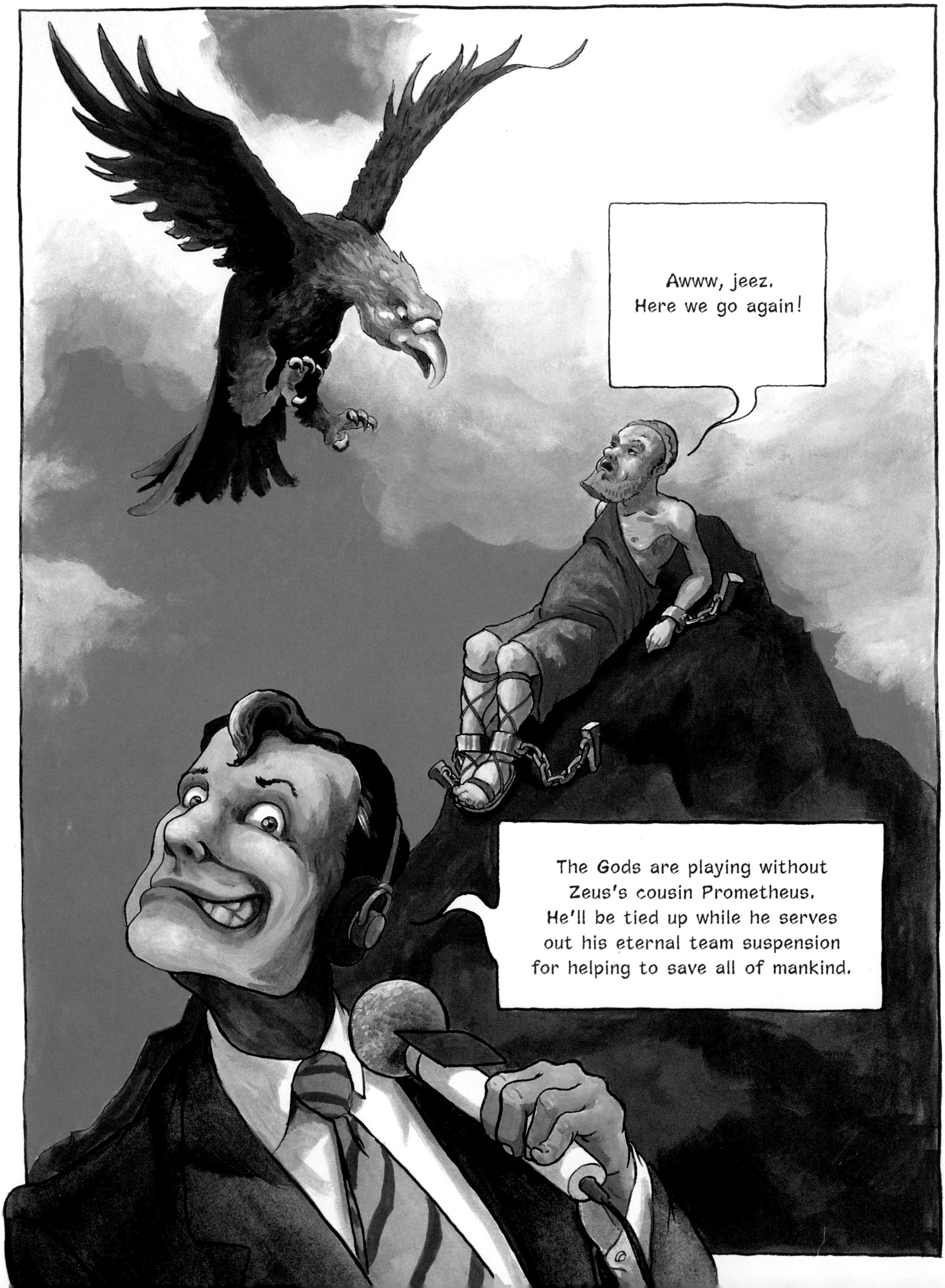
Awww, jeez. Here we go again!
The Gods are playing without Zeus's cousin Prometheus. He'll be tied up while he serves out his eternal team suspension for helping to save all of mankind.

The Mortals inbound the ball.
Achilles carries it over half-court.
He passes to Jason on the low post.
Poseidon is giving him all kinds of trouble.
Jason slips to the basket.
Poseidon is summoning a great wave.

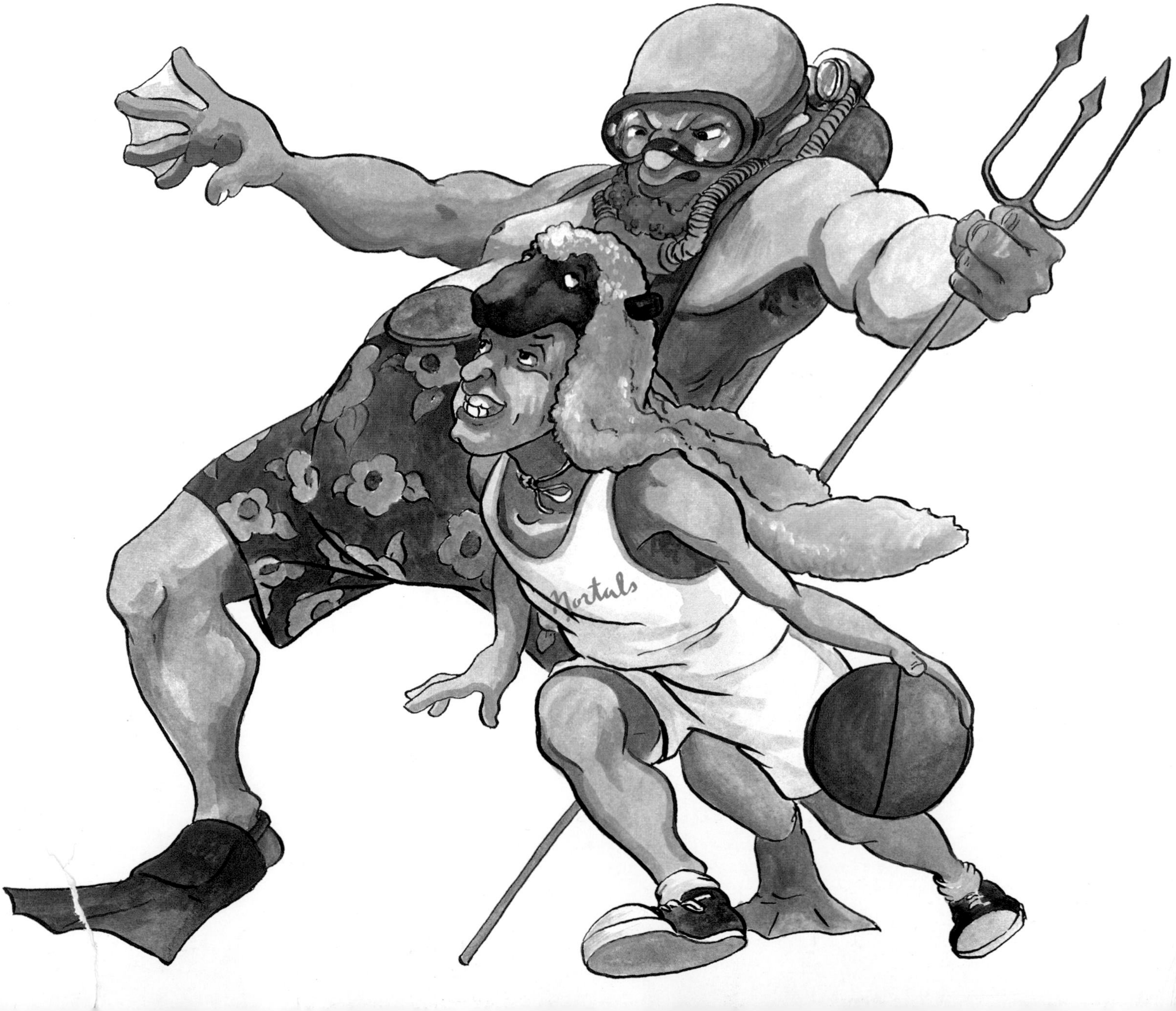
Mortals

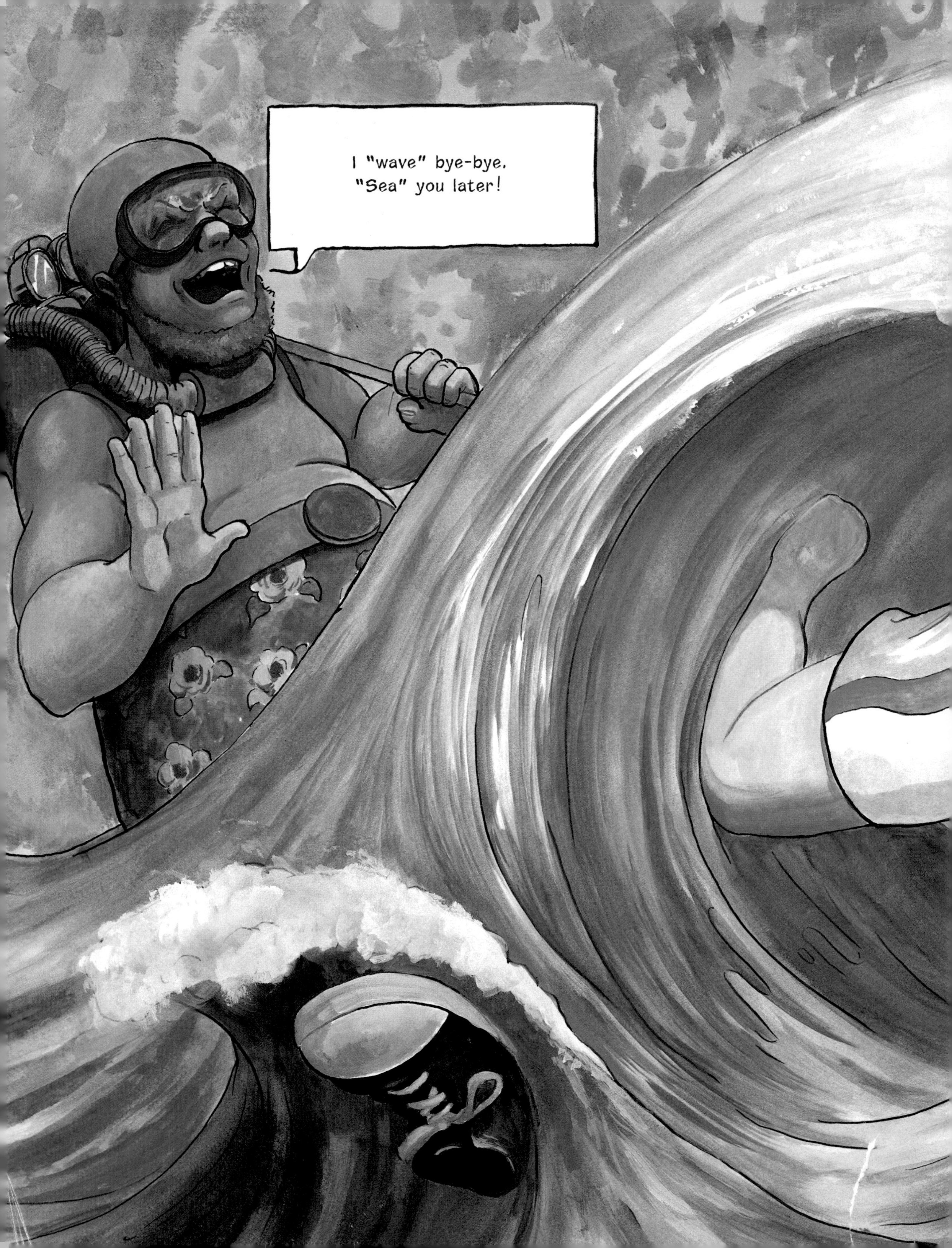
I "wave" bye-bye.
"Sea" you later!

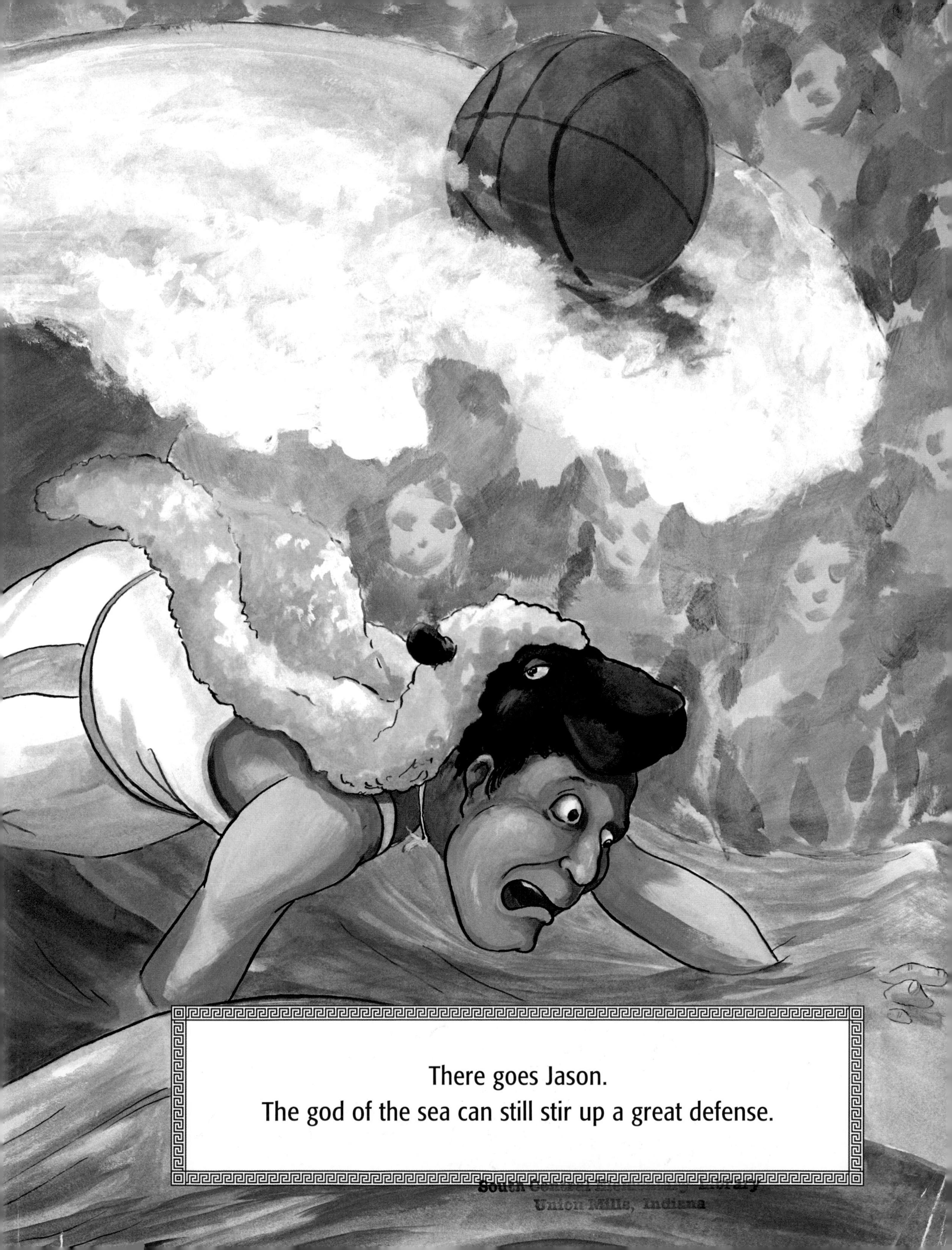

There goes Jason.
The god of the sea can still stir up a great defense.

Zeus has dried the sea and the game's back on.
That's Hades with the ball. He's at the top of the key.
What's this? He's opening a hole just under the basket.
All the players on team Mortal have fallen in.
Hades scores an easy two.

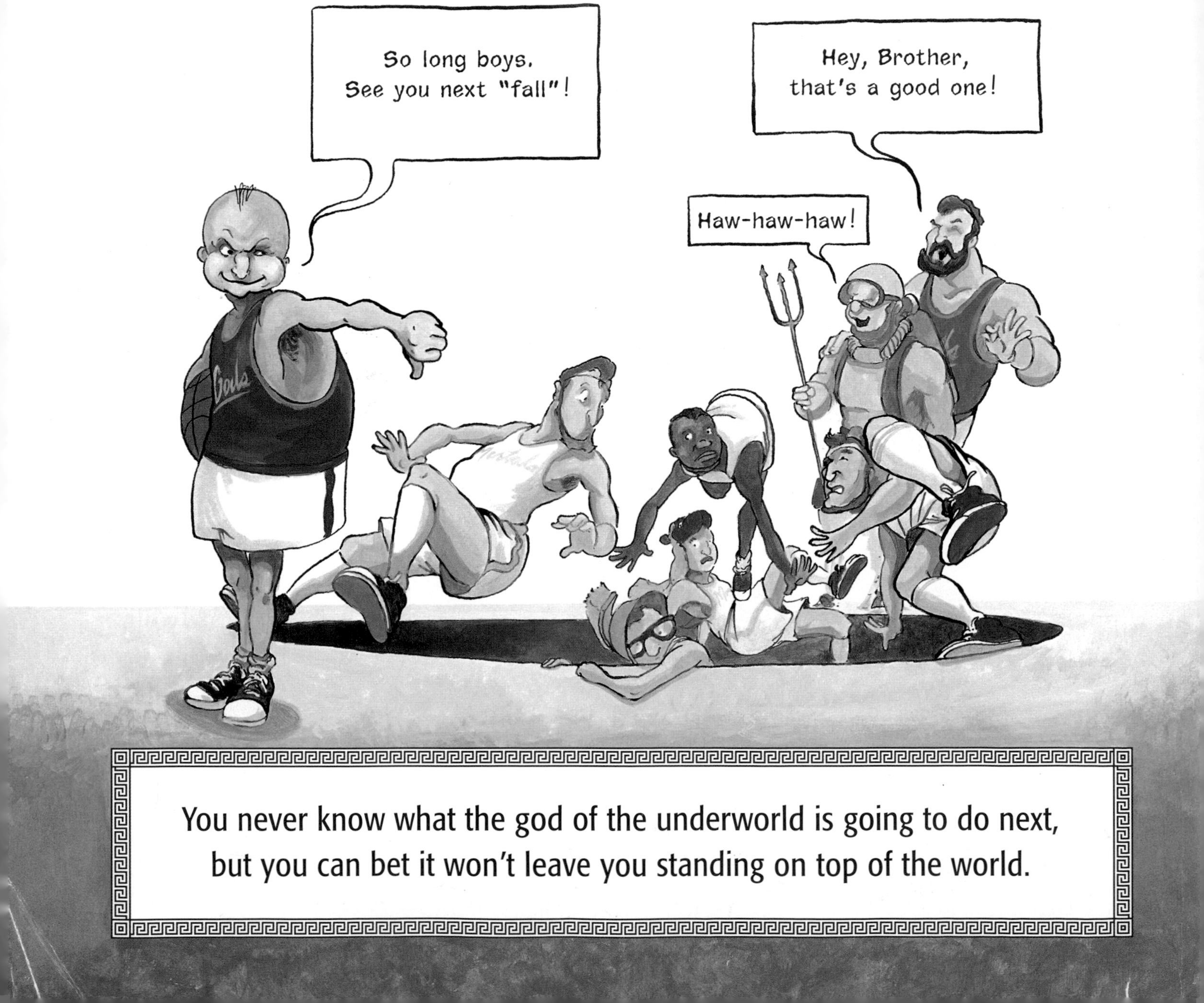
So long boys.
See you next "fall"!
Hey, Brother,
that's a good one!
Haw-haw-haw!

You never know what the god of the underworld is going to do next,
but you can bet it won't leave you standing on top of the world.

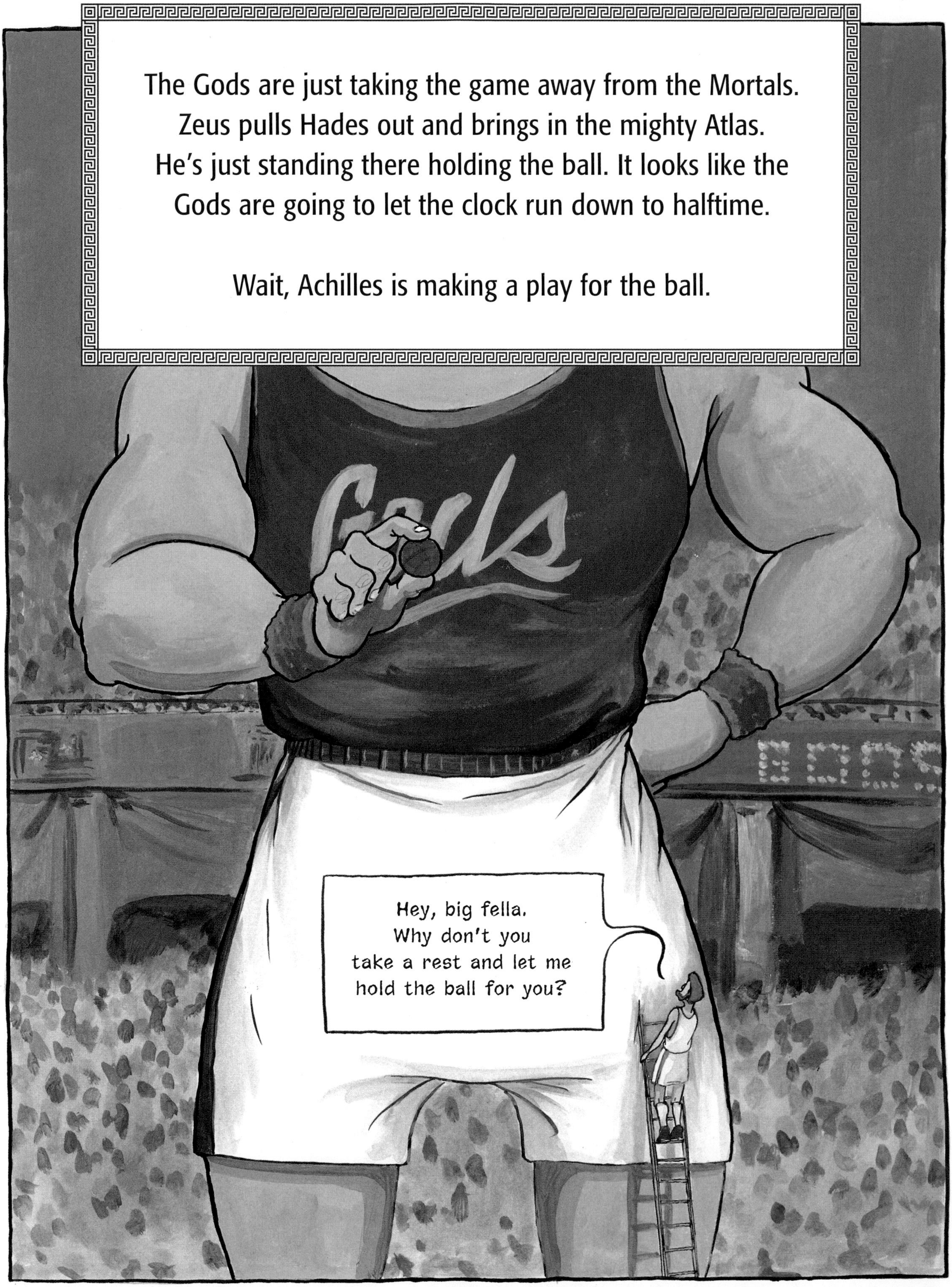
The Gods are just taking the game away from the Mortals. Zeus pulls Hades out and brings in the mighty Atlas. He's just standing there holding the ball. It looks like the Gods are going to let the clock run down to halftime.
Wait, Achilles is making a play for the ball.
Hey, big fella. Why don't you take a rest and let me hold the ball for you?

Atlas may be big. He may be strong.
But he's not very bright.
With just seconds left,
Atlas gives the ball to Achilles.
He shoots. He scores.
Just as the buzzer sounds for halftime.

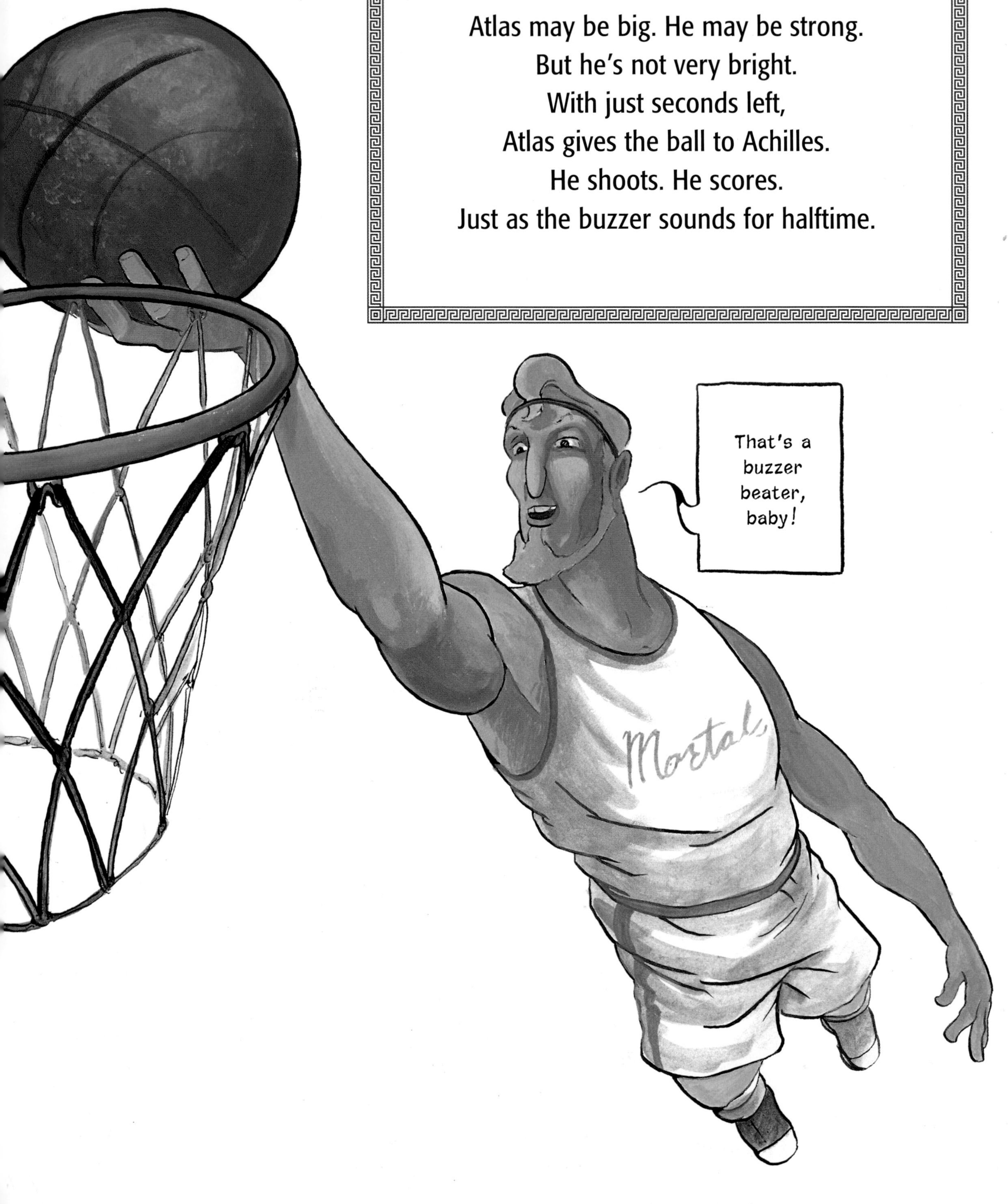
That's a buzzer beater, baby!
Mortals

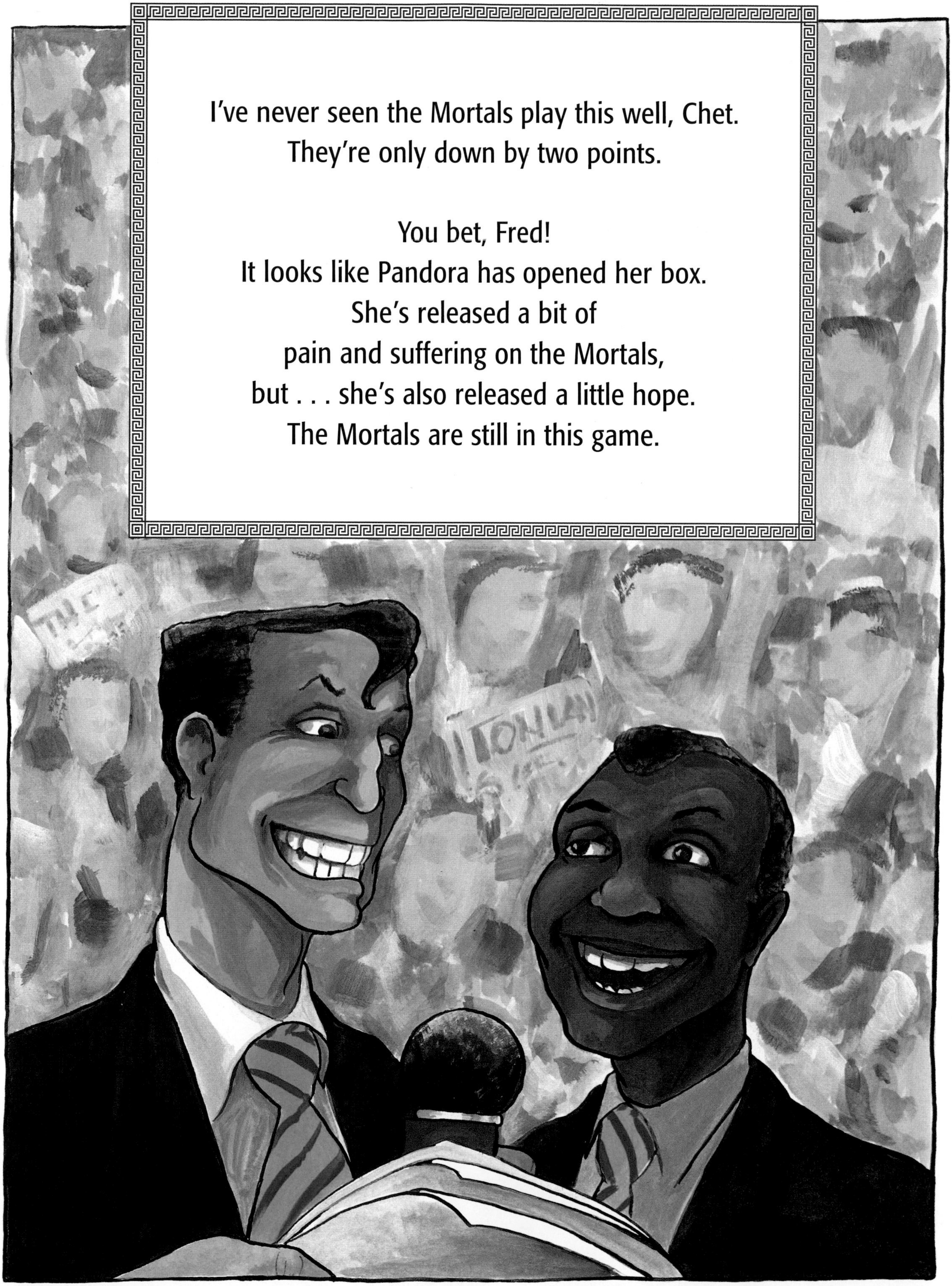
I've never seen the Mortals play this well, Chet.
They're only down by two points.
You bet, Fred!
It looks like Pandora has opened her box.
She's released a bit of
pain and suffering on the Mortals,
but . . . she's also released a little hope.
The Mortals are still in this game.

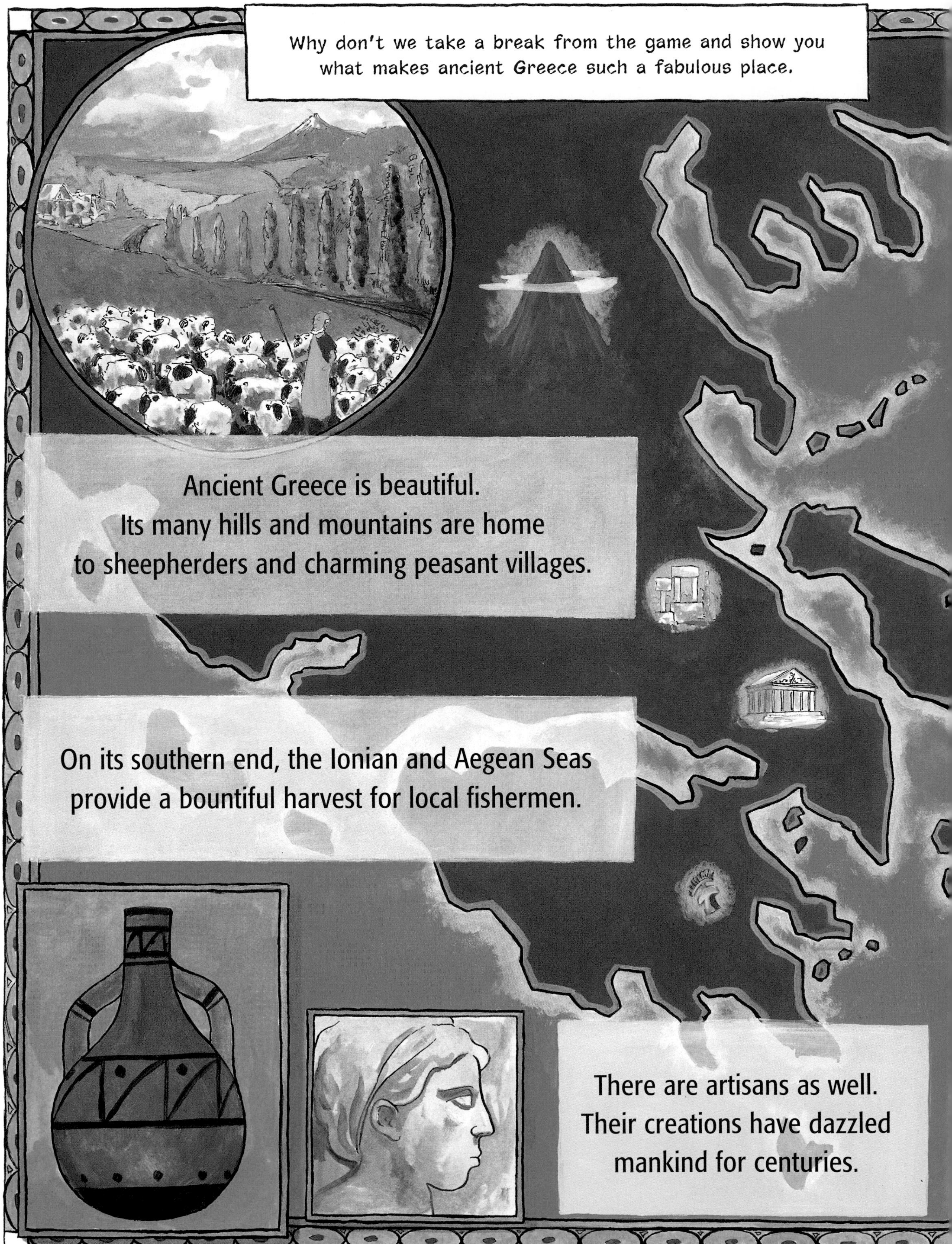

Why don't we take a break from the game and show you what makes ancient Greece such a fabulous place.
Ancient Greece is beautiful. Its many hills and mountains are home to sheepherders and charming peasant villages.
On its southern end, the Ionian and Aegean Seas provide a bountiful harvest for local fishermen.
There are artisans as well. Their creations have dazzled mankind for centuries.

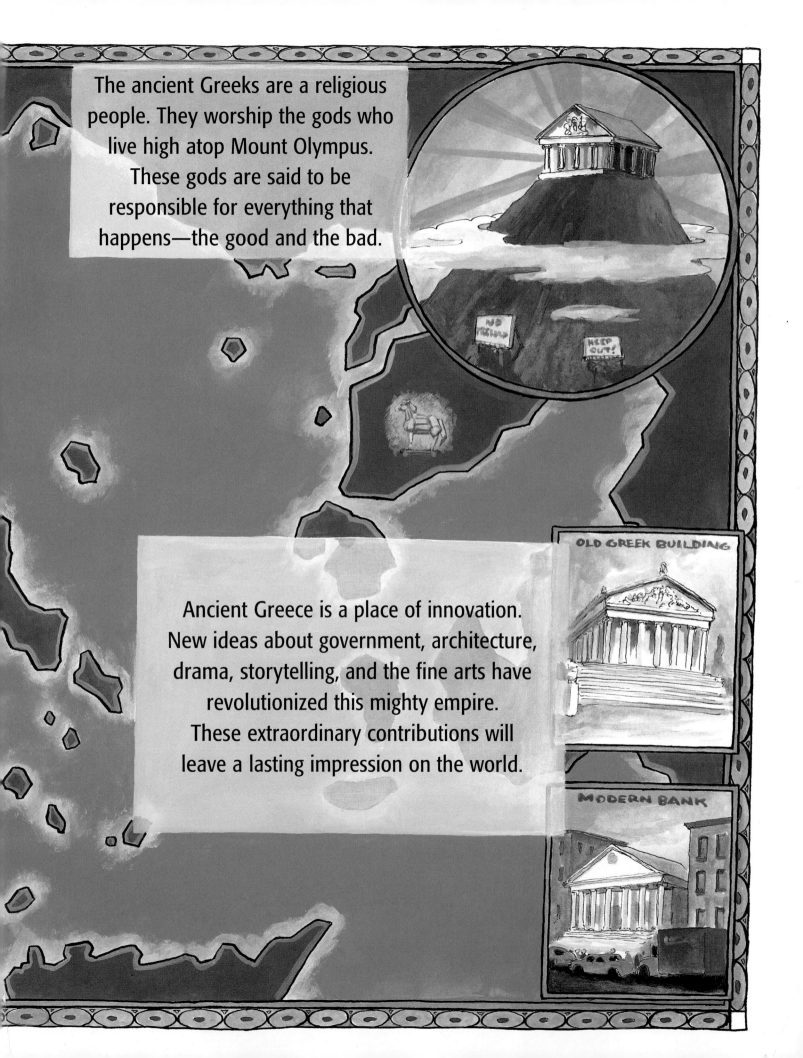

The ancient Greeks are a religious people. They worship the gods who live high atop Mount Olympus. These gods are said to be responsible for everything that happens—the good and the bad.

Ancient Greece is a place of innovation. New ideas about government, architecture, drama, storytelling, and the fine arts have revolutionized this mighty empire. These extraordinary contributions will leave a lasting impression on the world.

OLD GREEK BUILDING

MODERN BANK

Thanks, Chet. That was fascinating.
Well, the Gods are back on the court,
and we're about to start the second half of today's game.
Look for the Gods to overpower the Mortals this half.
Zeus doesn't take losing very well.
I'm sure he's got a few tricks up his tunic.

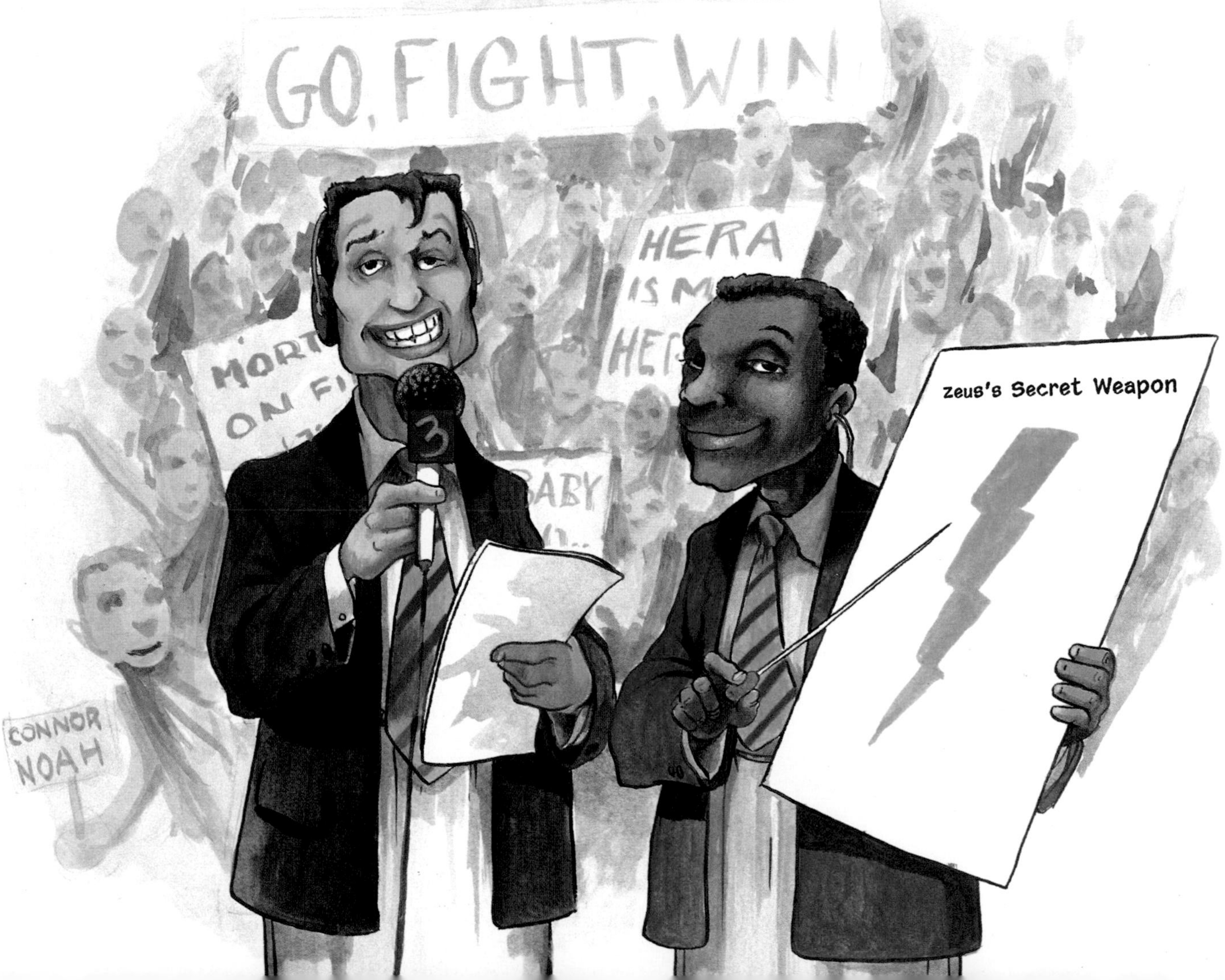
GO, FIGHT, WIN
HERA IS M HE
Zeus's Secret Weapon
CONNOR NOAH

The referee wants to start the game,
but the Mortals are nowhere to be seen.
Wait, what's this?
Why, it's a large wooden horse.
The beautiful Helen of Troy is pulling the horse to
the Gods' end of the court. She's talking with the Gods.

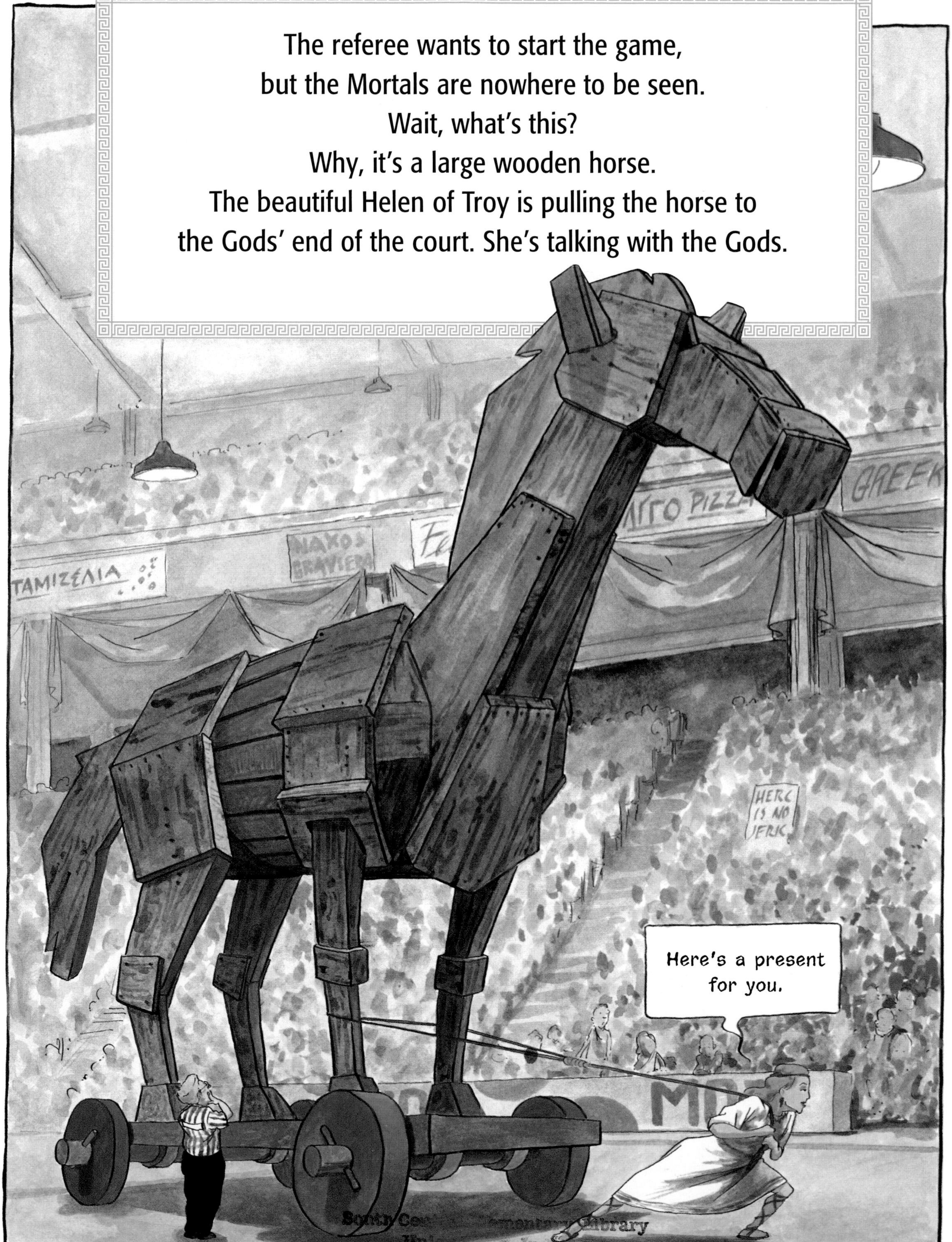
Here's a present for you.
HERC IS NO JERK
GREEK

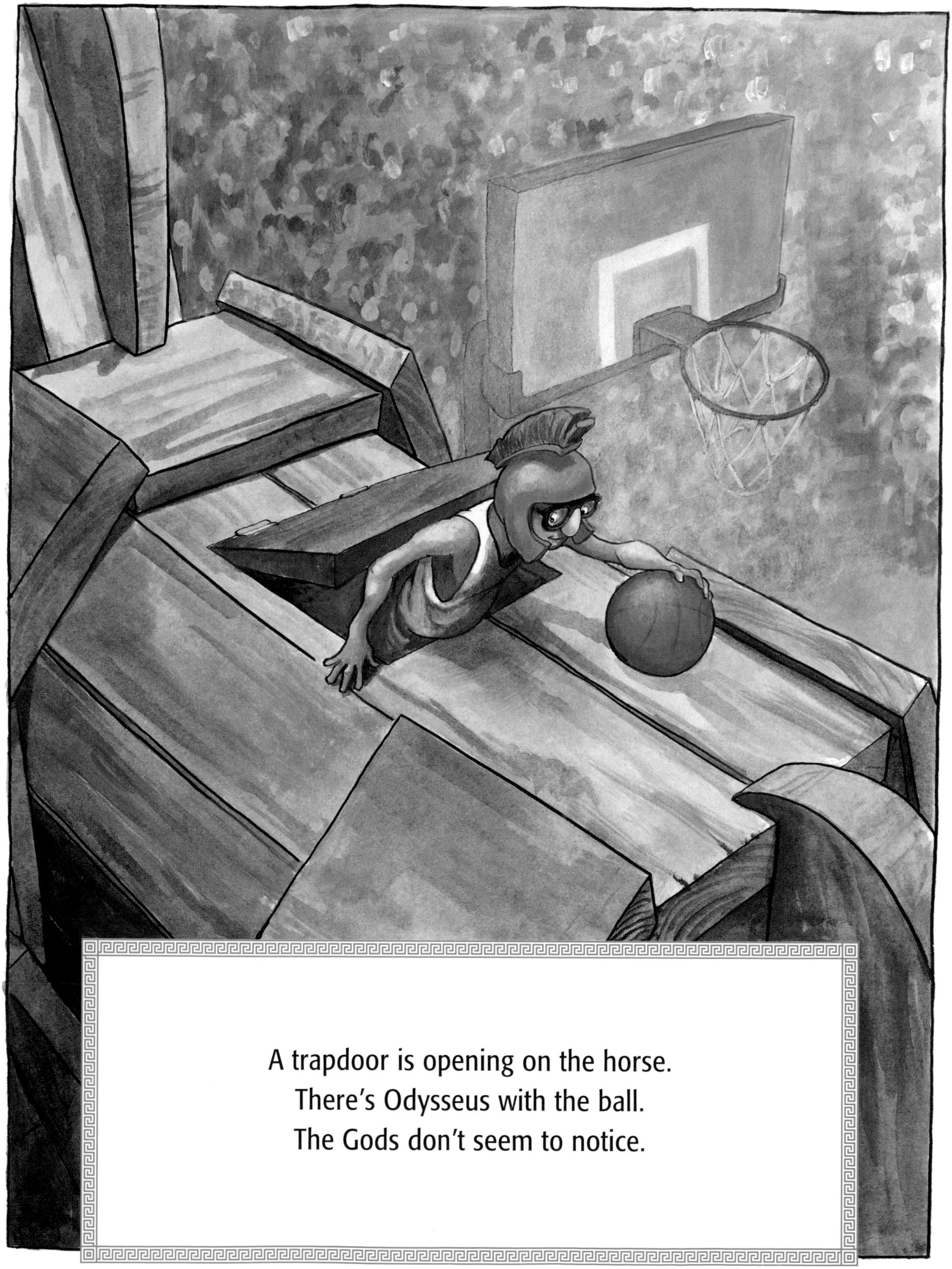

A trapdoor is opening on the horse.
There's Odysseus with the ball.
The Gods don't seem to notice.

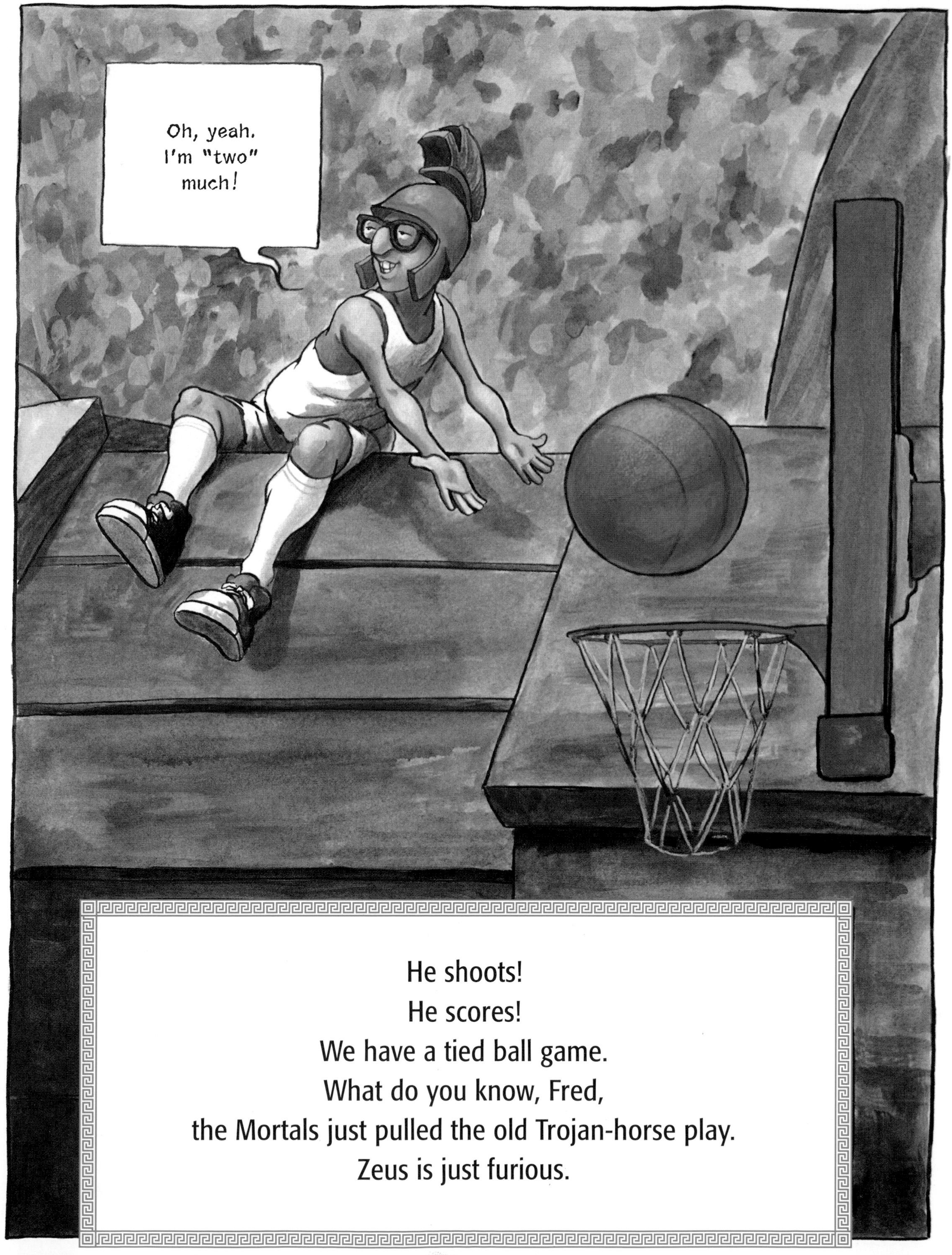
Oh, yeah. I'm "two" much!

He shoots!
He scores!
We have a tied ball game.
What do you know, Fred,
the Mortals just pulled the old Trojan-horse play.
Zeus is just furious.

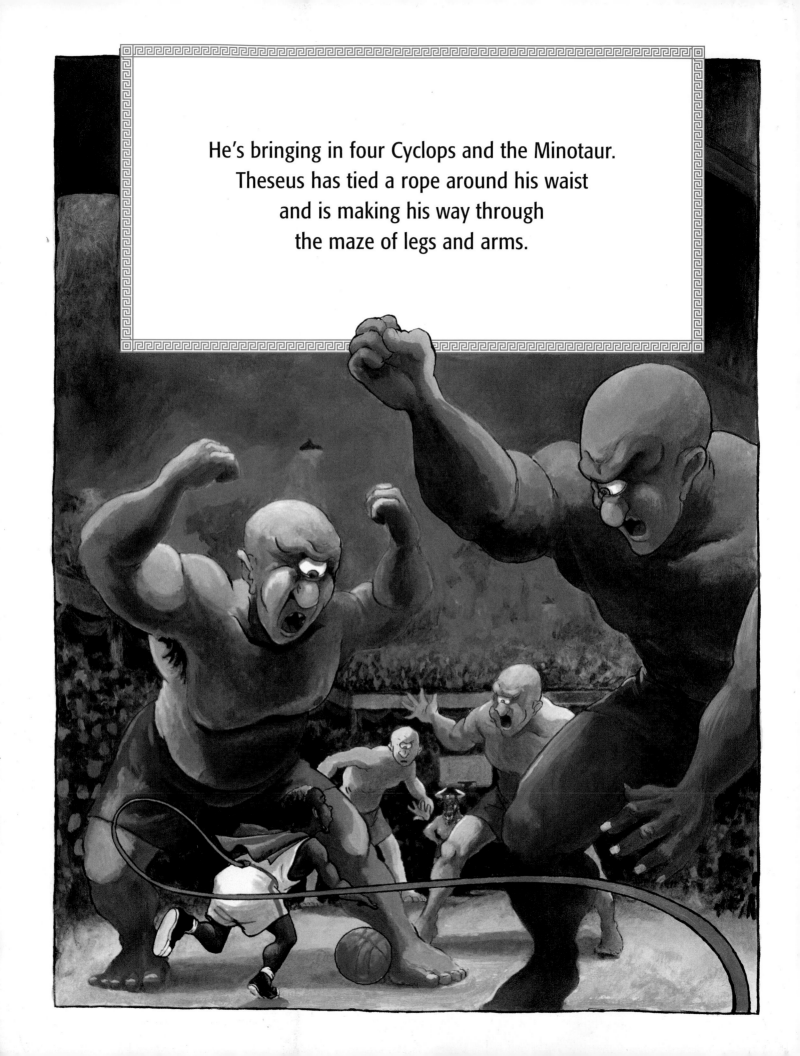

He's bringing in four Cyclops and the Minotaur.
Theseus has tied a rope around his waist
and is making his way through
the maze of legs and arms.

He reaches the Minotaur,
he leaps up and slams home the ball!
Theseus has just defeated
the Minotaur.
The Mortals have
taken the lead!
It looks like nothing can
stop them now!

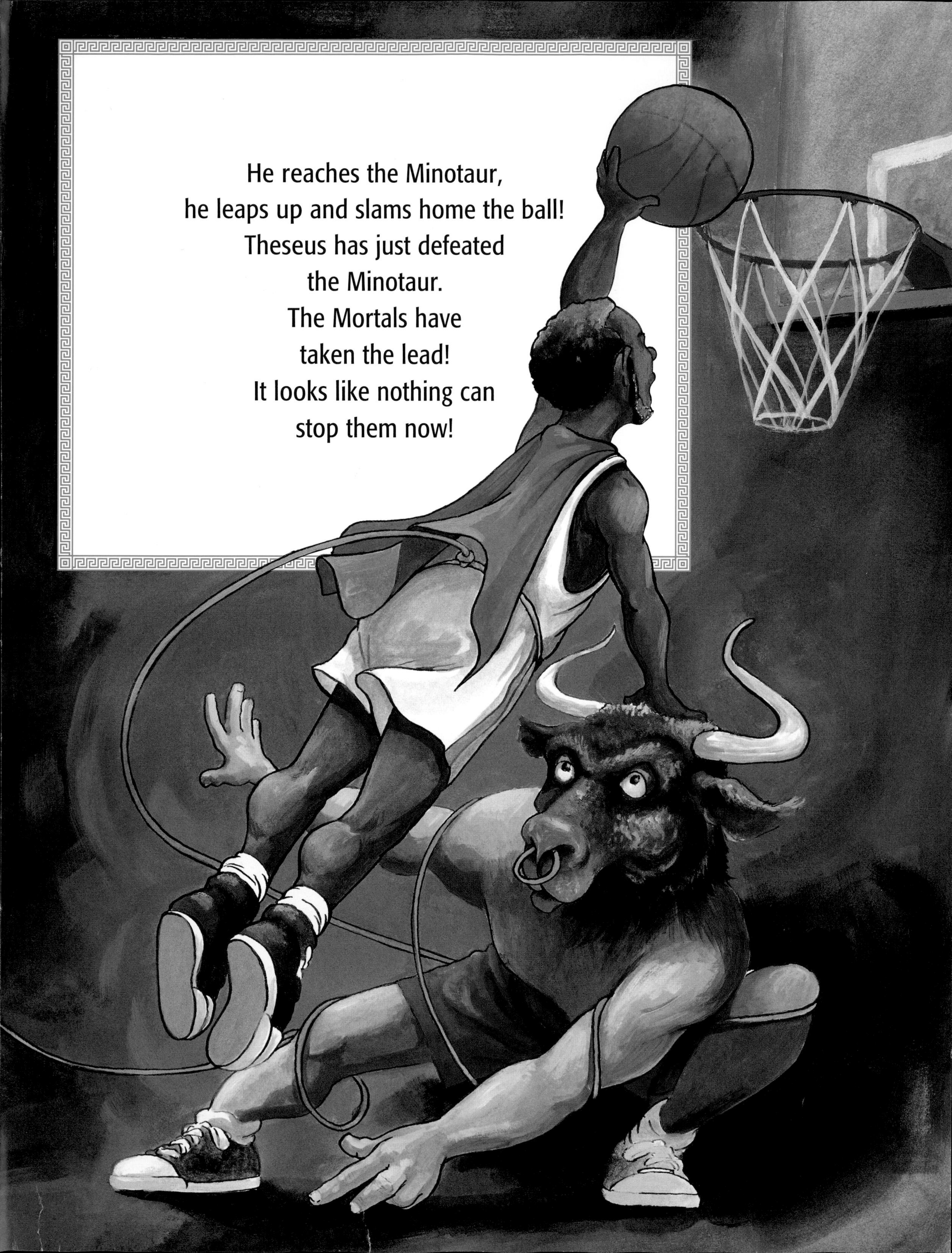

Wait a minute. It looks like Zeus has had enough.
He grabs the ball.
He's raising it above his head.
He's opening up the heavens.
Hail, thunder, and lightning are raining down on the court.
The Mortals are running for cover.

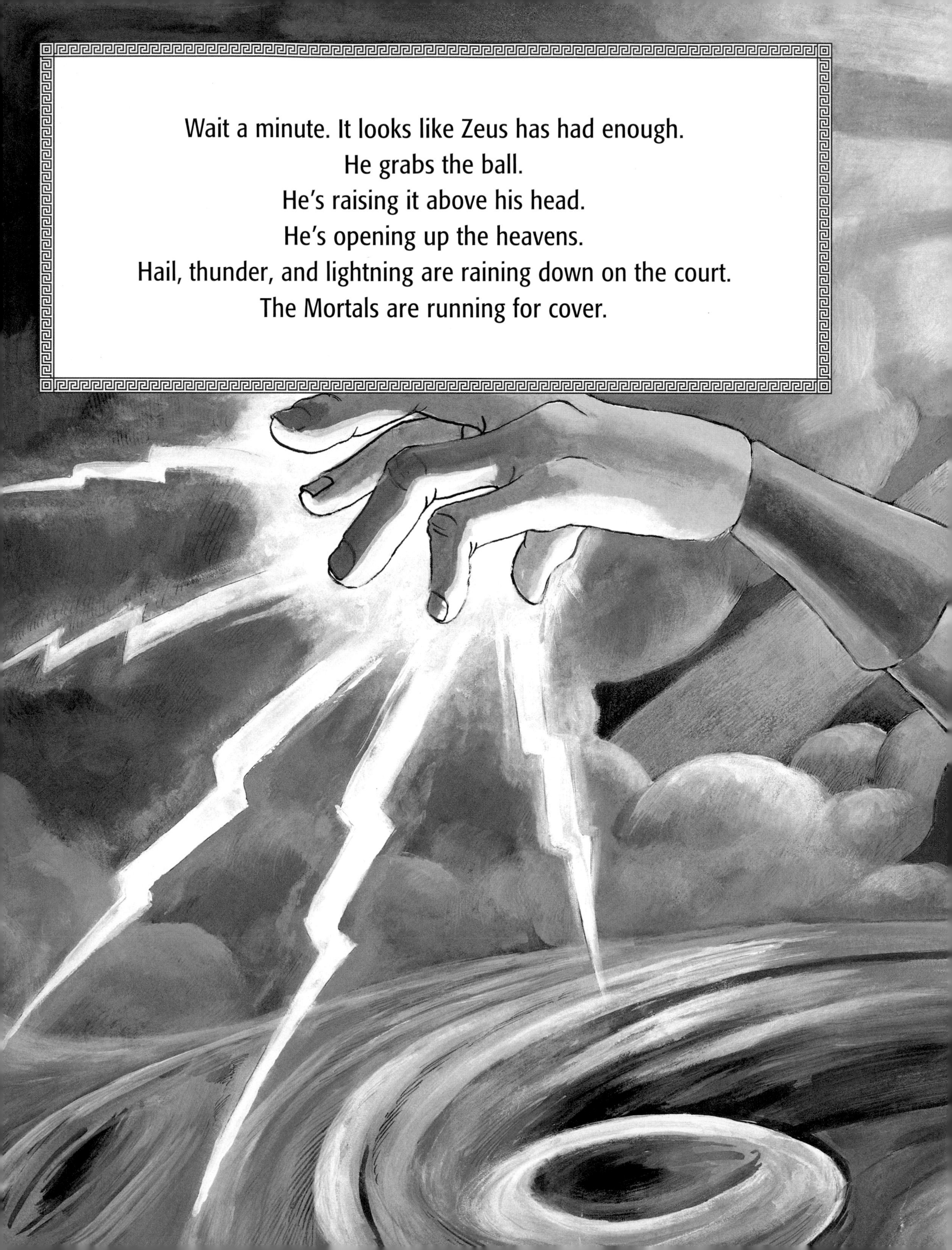

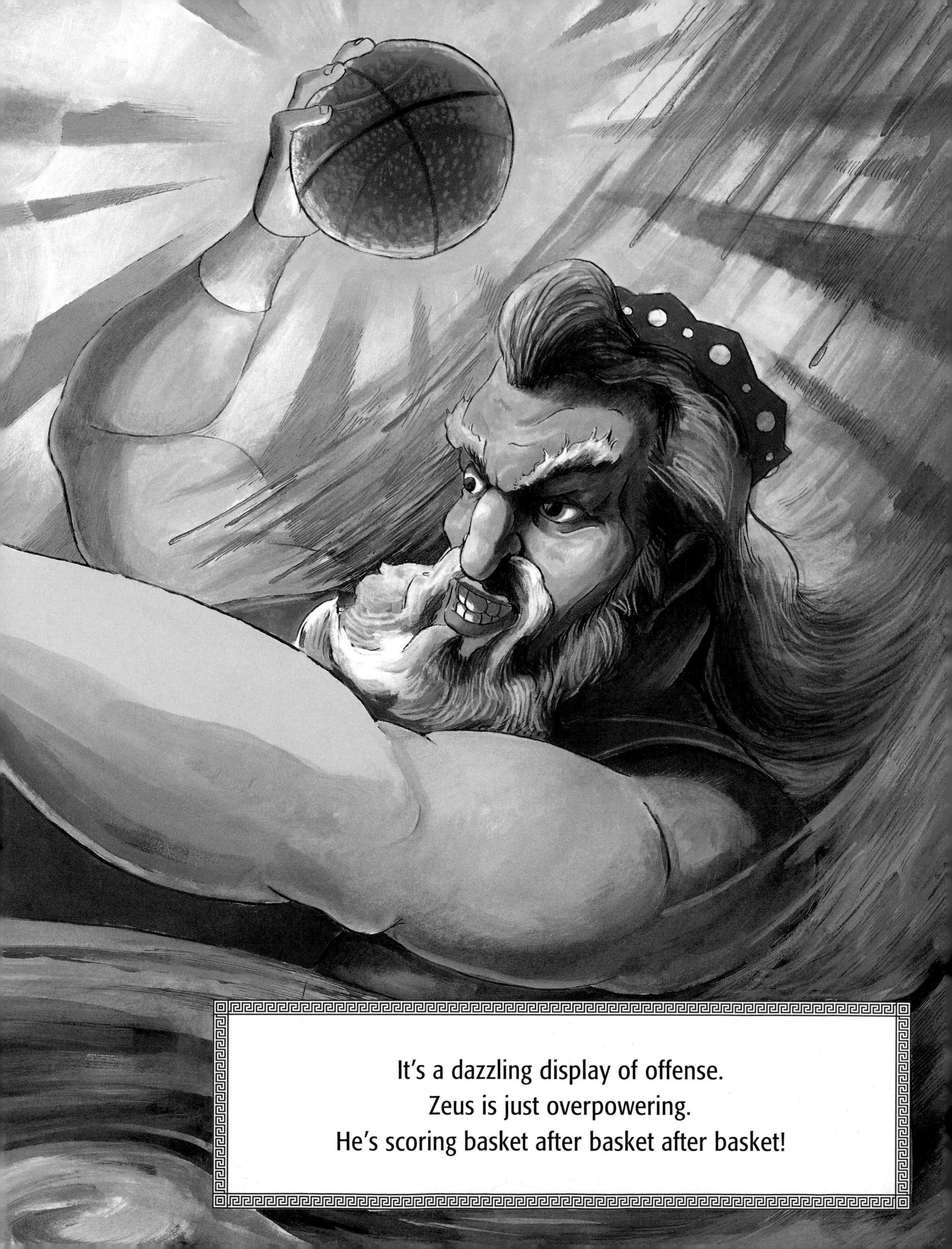

It's a dazzling display of offense.
Zeus is just overpowering.
He's scoring basket after basket after basket!

Well, folks, the goddess of victory—
Nike herself—is flapping her wings,
and this game is history.
The Mortals really gave it their all,
but you can mark it down as yet another win
for the all-powerful Gods of Mount Olympus.
Final score: Gods: 2,678,352, Mortals: 6.
Join us next week when the Mythical Monsters of the
Sea play the Mythical Beasts of the Land.

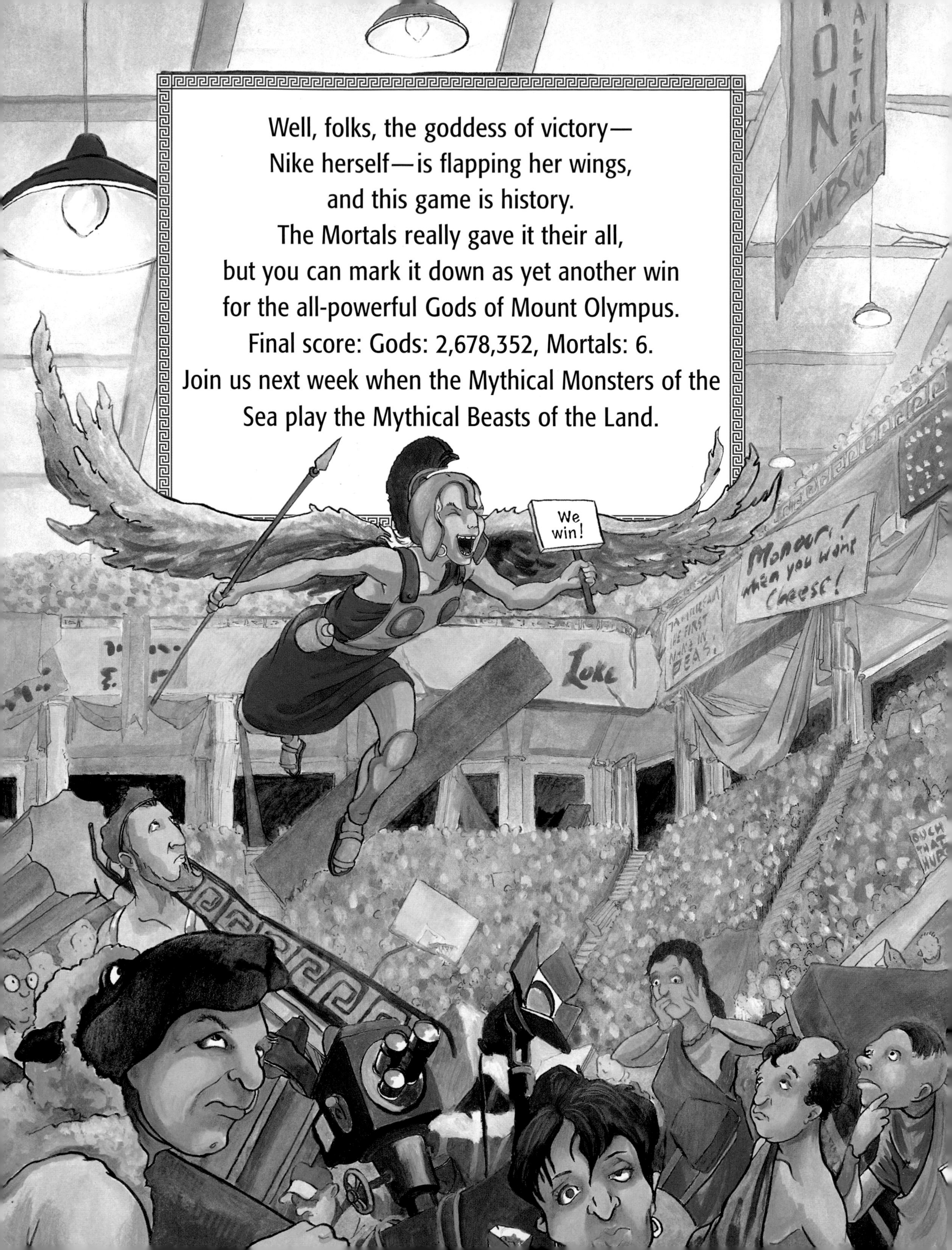
We win!

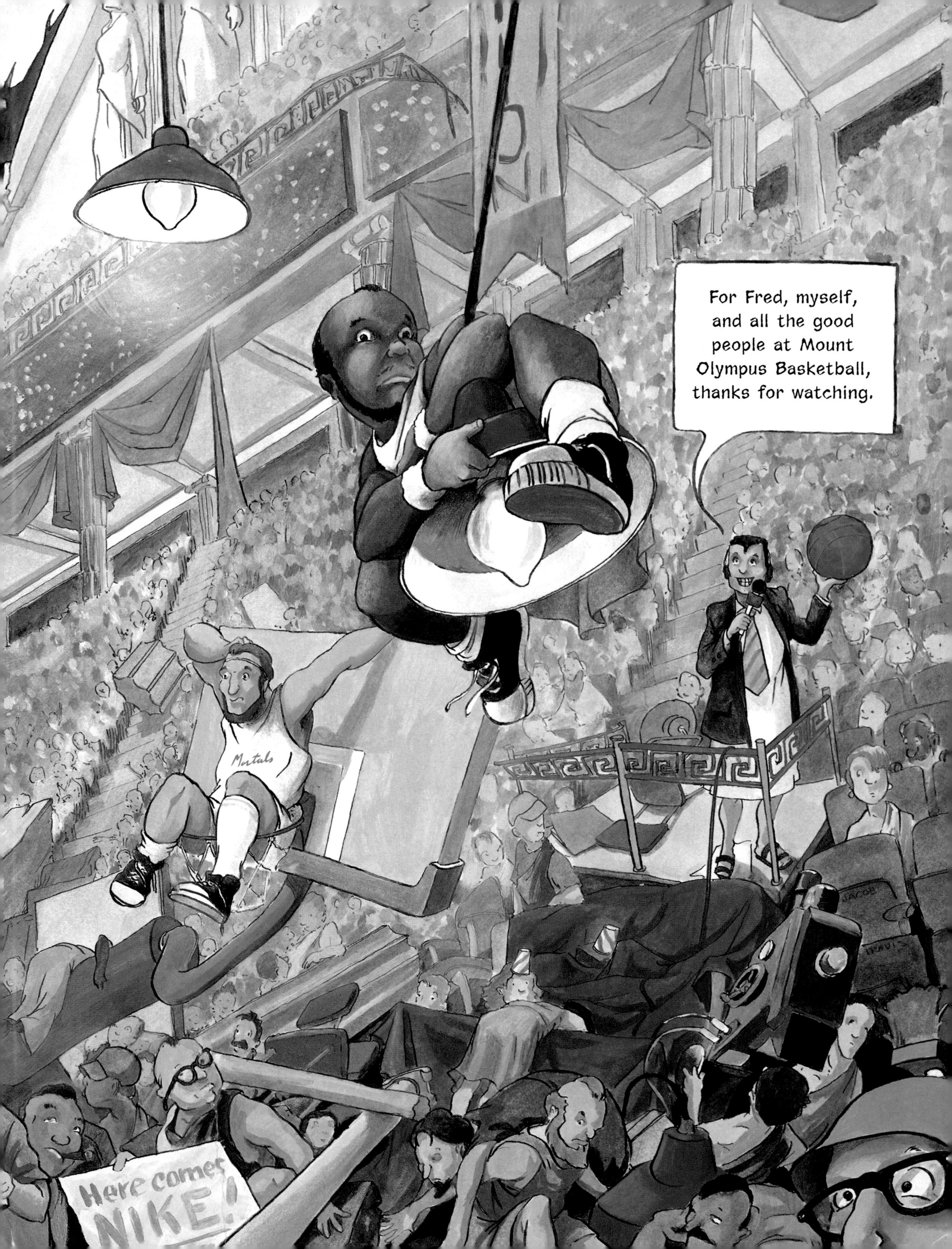
For Fred, myself, and all the good people at Mount Olympus Basketball, thanks for watching.
Here comes NIKE!

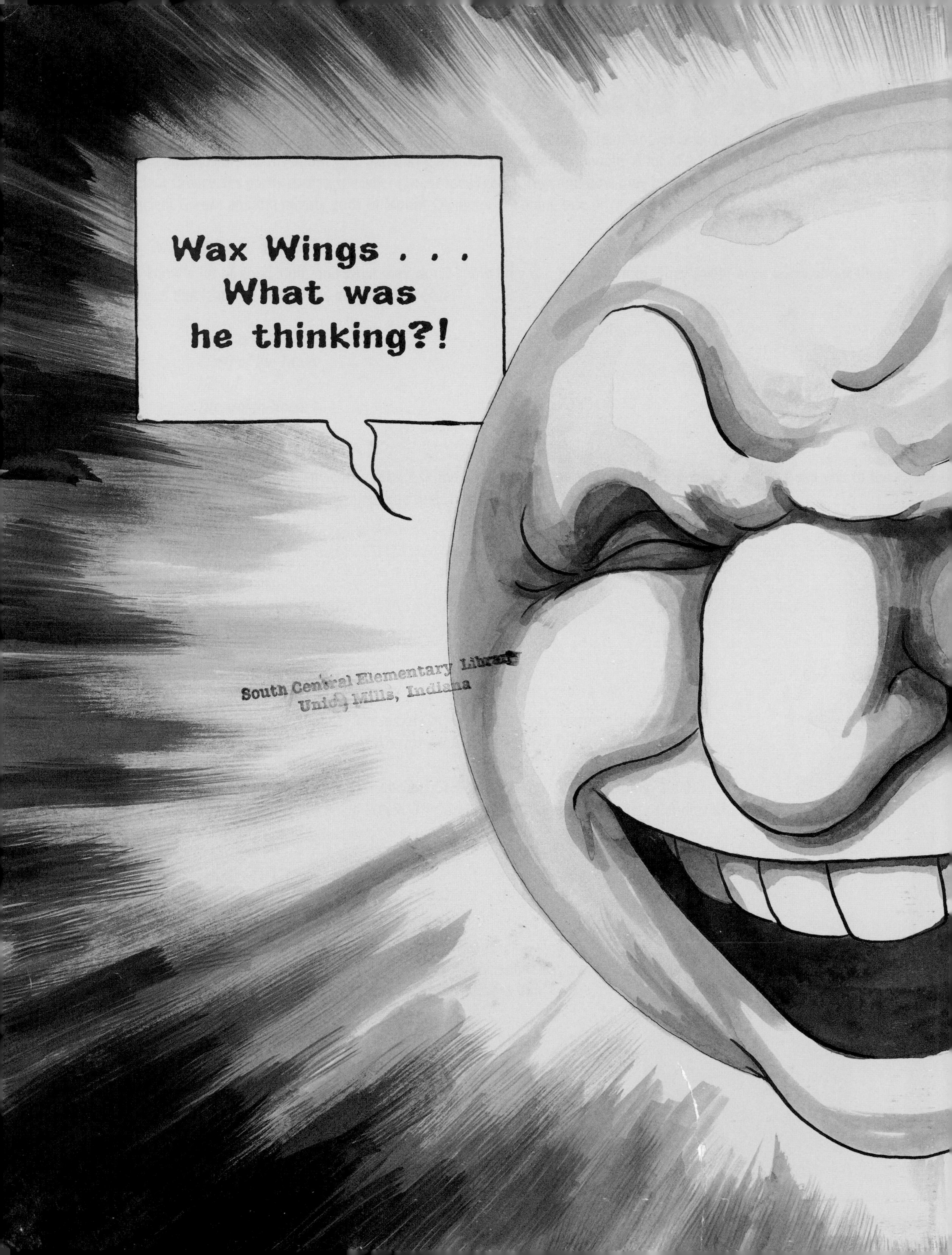
Wax Wings . . . What was he thinking?!